PRIME MERIDIAN

PRIME MERIDIAN

SILVIA MORENO-GARCIA

Published by Innsmouth Free Press
Vancouver, BC Canada
http://innsmouthfreepress.com

ISBN paperback 978-1-927990-21-6
ISBN e-book 978-1-927990-22-3

Cover artwork: istockphoto MATJAZ SLANIC, KrisCole

Layout and cover design: Silvia Moreno-Garcia

INTRODUCTION

I think I first came across the work of Silvia Moreno-Garcia in the virtual pages of an online magazine called *Futurismic*. Her story, "Maquech," caught me immediately, with that sense one gets of having made an important new discovery, as though the story itself were a "jewel-encrusted beetle," like the one described within it. Already in that story, one could see the seeds of work to come. The milieu of Mexico City, for instance, written not as some faux-exotic Otherness for the consumption of North American armchair tourists, but as a place which is lived in, which is worn and comfortable and mundane, in which the science-fictional trappings evolve and adapt naturally.

Since then, I've had the good fortune to reprint the story in my *Apex Book of World SF 2* anthology and, in turn, appeared in one of Silvia's own anthologies, *Fungi*. Most recently, what began as a joke on Twitter to come up with the stuffiest possible name for a literary magazine — we settled on *The Jewish Mexican Literary Review* — became a reality with two issues already published at the time of writing. And the legendary founder of that esteemed journal — one Nahum (Eduard) Landmann — makes, in turn, a cameo appearance in this story. *Prime Meridian* is an... excuse me... *prime* example of Silvia's work. If *Signal to Noise*, her 2015 debut novel, is a paean to — or perhaps lament for — the pop music of an 80s childhood in Mexico City, then *Prime Meridian* returns to another great love: the movies. The real Mars, one could say, is a construct of the imagination.

Forget the lifeless planet that's actually there. The real Mars is a place of yearning, the promise of escape, an Otherland that has caught the collective imagination for centuries. "There is air here," Silvia writes. For this isn't our Mars, but the movie planet of "EXT. MARS SURFACE — DAY."

But if Mars is a land of wish fulfillment and escape, the people who live in Silvia's future Mexico are stranded much as we are, in the here and now of drudgery and work, relationships and the minuet of the everyday, having to make a living, barely getting time to dream.

In this, Silvia echoes, not the majority of SF writers with their shiny futures and ragged heroes, but that most unlikely of novelists, the late Philip K. Dick, for whom the future was only ever inhabited by the little people, by people like us, and for whom Mars represented the same sort of escape. It is an escape from the mundane into the fantastical, but is escape possible? Is it even desirable?

The novella, I've long felt, is the perfect form of story. Long enough to submerge us in its world, to make us care about its characters, yet just short enough to be stripped of the excess fat of novels, short enough to be focused and lean. In this deeply humanistic story of people living in a present/future at just a few angles different from ours, Silvia has crafted a quiet masterpiece.

I feel privileged to have read it early and I'm envious that you get to read it now, for the first time. I loved it — and I'm sure you'll feel the same.

Lavie Tidhar, 2017

Why did I have to poison myself with love?

— *Aelita, or The Decline of Mars*, Alexei Tolstoi

*

Una ciudad deshecha, gris, monstruosa

— "Alta traición," José Emilio Pacheco

1

The subway station was a dud. Both of its entrances had once again been commandeered by a street gang that morning, which meant you'd have to pay a small 'fee' in order to catch your train. Amelia was tempted to fork over the cash, but you never knew if these assholes were also going to help themselves to your purse, your cell phone, and whatever the hell else they wanted.

That meant she had to choose between a shared ride and the bus. Amelia didn't like either option. The bus was cheap. It would also take forever for it to reach Coyoacán. The car could also take a while, depending on how many people hailed it, but it would no doubt move faster.

Amelia was supposed to meet Fernanda for lunch the next day and she needed to ensure she had enough money to pay for her meal. Fernanda was loaded, and odds were she'd cover it all, but Amelia didn't want to risk it in case Fernanda wasn't feeling generous.

The most sensible thing to do, considering this, was to take the bus. Problem was, she had the booking and if she didn't check in by five o'clock, she'd be penalized, a percentage of her earnings deducted. The damned app had a geolocator function. Amelia couldn't lie and claim she'd reached the house on time.

Amelia gave the gang members standing by the subway station's entrance a long glare and took out her cell phone.

Five minutes later, her ride arrived. She was glad to discover there was only one other person in the car. Last time she'd taken a shared ride, she sat together with four people, including a woman with a baby, the cries of the child deafening Amelia.

Amelia boarded the car and gave the other passenger a polite nod. The man hardly returned it. He was wearing a gray suit and carried a briefcase, which he clutched with one hand while he held up his cell phone in the other. You heard all these stories about how the ride shares were dangerous — you could get into a car and be mugged, express kidnapped, or raped — but Amelia wasn't going to pay for a damned secure taxi and this guy, at least, didn't look like he was going to pull a gun on her. He was too busy yakking on the phone.

They made good progress despite the usual insanity of Mexico City's traffic. In Europe, there were automated cars roaming the cities, but here drivers still had a job. They couldn't automate that, not with the chaotic fuckery of the roads.

Mars is home to the tallest mountain in the solar system. Olympus Mons, 21 km high and 600 km in diameter, she told herself as the driver honked the horn. Sometimes, she repeated the Mandarin words she knew, but it was mostly facts about the Red Planet. To remind herself it was real, it existed, it was there.

Once they approached the old square in Coyoacán, Amelia jumped out of the car. No point in staying inside; the vehicle moved at a snail's pace. The cobblestone streets in this borough were never made to bear the multitudes that now walked through the once-small village.

The square that marked the center of old Coyoacán was chock-full of street vendors frying churros and gorditas, or offering bags emblazoned with the face of Frida Kahlo and acrylic rebozos made in China. Folkloric bullshit.

Amelia took a side street, where the traditional pulquerias had been substituted with fusion restaurants. Korean-Mexican. French-Mexican. Whatever-Mexican. Mexican-Mexican was never enough. A couple of more blocks and she reached Lucía's home with five minutes to spare, thank-fucking-God.

Lucía's house was not an ordinary house, but a full-fledge casona, a historical marvel that looked like it was out of a movie, with wrought iron bars on the windows and an interior patio crammed with potted plants. The inside was much of the same: rustic tables and hand-painted talavera. It screamed Colonial, provincial, nostalgia and also fake. There was an artificial, too-calculated, too-overdone quality to each and every corner of the house, an unintended clue that the owner had once been an actress.

Amelia knew the drill. She went into the living room with its enormous screen and sat on one of the couches. Lucía was already there. The woman drank nothing except mineral water with a wedge of lime. The first time Amelia had visited her, she had made the mistake of asking for a Diet Coke, which earned her a raised eyebrow and a mineral water, because fuck you, Lucía Madrigal said what you drank and what you ate (nothing, most times, although twice, little bowls with pomegranate seeds had been placed on the table by the couches).

That day, there were no pomegranates, only the mineral water and Lucía, dressed in a bright green dress with a matching turban, the kind Elizabeth Taylor wore in the 70s. That had been Lucía's heyday and she had not acclimated to modern dress styles, preferring tacky drama to demure senior citizen clothes.

"Today, we are going to watch my second movie. The Mars picture. I was quite young when this came out in '65, so it's not one of my best roles," Lucía declared with such aplomb one might have believed she had been a real actress, instead of a middling starlet who got lucky and married a filthy rich politician.

Amelia nodded. She had little interest in Lucía's movies, but her job was not to offer commentary. It was to simply sit and watch. Sometimes, it was to sit and listen. Lucía liked to go on about the film stars she'd met in decades past or the autobiography she was writing. As long as Amelia kept her eyes open and her mouth shut, she'd get a good rating on Friendrr and her due payment, minus the 20% commission for the broker. There were other apps that functioned without a broker, but those were less reliable. You might arrive for your Friendrr session and discover the client was an absolute sleaze who wouldn't pay. Friendrr vetted the clients, asked for deposits, and charged more, which was good news.

The movie was short and confusing, as if it had been rewritten halfway through the production. The first half focused on a space ranger sent to check out a Martian outpost manned by a scientist and his lovely daughter. Lucía played the daughter, who wore 'futuristic' silver miniskirts. For its first half-hour, it played as a tame romance. Then space pirates, who looked suspiciously like they were wearing discarded clothes from a Mexican Revolution film, invaded the outpost. The pirates were under the command of a Space Queen who was obviously evil, due to the plunging neckline of her costume.

"It doesn't much look like the real Mars, I suppose," Lucía mused, "but then, I prefer it this way. The real Mars is bland compared to the one the set designer imagined. Have you seen the pictures of the colonies?"

"Yes," Amelia said, and although she knew only monosyllabics were required of her, she went on. "I want to go there, soon."

"To the Martian colonies?"

Lucía looked at the young woman. The actress had indulged in plastic surgery at several points during the 90s and her face seemed waxy. Time could not be stopped, though, and she had long abandoned attempts at surgery, botox and peels. What remained of her was like the core of a dead tree. Her eyebrows were non-existent, drawn with aplomb and a brown pencil. She perpetually sported a half-amused expression and a necklace, which she inevitably toyed with.

"Well, I suppose people are meant to go places," Lucía said. "But those colonies on Mars, they look as antiseptic and exciting as a box of baby wipes. Everything is white. Who ever heard of white as an exciting color?"

There was irony in this comment, since the movie they had just watched was in black-and-white, but Amelia nodded. Half an hour later, she took the bus back home.

When Amelia walked into the apartment, the television was on. Her sister and her youngest niece were on the couch, watching a reality TV show. Her other niece was probably on the bed, with her phone. Since there were two bedrooms and Amelia had to share a room with one of the girls, the only place where she could summon a modicum of privacy was the bathroom, but when she zipped toward there after a quiet 'hello,' Marta looked at her.

"I hope you're not thinking of taking a shower," her sister said. "Last month's water bill came in. It's very high."

"That's the fault of the people in the building next door," Amelia said. "You know they steal water from the tinacos."

"You take forever in the shower. Your hair's not even dirty. Why would you need to get in the shower?"

Amelia did not reply. She changed course, headed into the bedroom, and slipped under the covers. On the other bed, her niece played a game on her cell phone. Its repetitive bop-bop sound allowed for neither sleep nor coherent thoughts.

2

Amelia took her nieces to school, which meant an annoying elbowing in and out of a crowded bus, plus the masterful avoiding of men who tried to touch her ass. Marta insisted that the girls needed to be picked up and dropped off from school, even though Karina was 11 and could catch the school transport together with her little sister, no problem. It was just a modest fee for this privilege.

Amelia thought Marta demanded she perform this task as a way to demonstrate her power.

When Amelia returned from dropping off the girls, she took the shower that had been forbidden her the previous night. Afterward, she cooked a quick meal for the family and left it in the refrigerator — this was another of the tasks she had to execute, along with the drop-offs and pick-ups. Again, she boarded a bus, squeezed tight next to two men, the smell of cheap cologne clogging her nostrils, and got off near the Diana.

Fernanda was characteristically laggard, strolling into the restaurant half an hour late. She did not apologize for the delay. She sat down, ordered a salad after reading the menu twice, and smiled at Amelia.

"I have met the most excellent massage therapist," Fernanda said. This was her favorite adjective. She had many, employed them generously. "He got rid of that pain in my back. I told you about it, didn't I? Between the shoulder blades. And the most excellent…."

She droned on. Fernanda and Amelia did not meet often anymore, but when they did, Amelia had to listen patiently about all the wonderful, amazing, super-awesome people Fernanda knew, the cool-brilliant-mega hobbies she was busying herself with, and the delightful-darling-divine trips she'd taken recently. It was pretty much the same structure as her visits with Lucía, the old woman discussing her movies while Amelia watched the ice cubes in her glass melt.

It made her feel cheap and irritated, but Fernanda footed their lunch bills and she had lent money to Amelia on previous occasions. Right now, she was wondering if she should ask for a bit of cash or bite her tongue.

Amelia, who didn't drink regularly in restaurants (who would with these prices?), ordered a martini to pass the time. Fernanda was already on her second one. She drank a lot but only when her husband wasn't looking. He was ugly, grouchy and wealthy. The last attribute was the only one that mattered to Fernanda.

"So, what are you doing now?" Fernanda asked. Her smile was blinding, her hair painted an off-putting shade of blonde, her dark roots showing. Not Brigitte Bardot — bouts of movie-watching with Lucía were giving Amelia a sense of film history — but a straw-like color that wasn't bold, just boring. Every woman of a certain age had that hair color. They'd copied it off a celebrity who had a nightly variety show. No brunettes on TV. Pale skin and fair hair were paramount.

"This and that," Amelia replied.

"You're not working? Don't tell me you're still doing that awful-terrible rent-a-friend thing," Fernanda said, looking surprised.

"Yes. Although, I wanted to ask if you hadn't heard of anything that might suit me…."

"Well… your field, it's not really my line of work," Fernanda replied.

Not that Fernanda had a line of work. As far as Amelia knew, all she did was stay married, her bills paid by her dick of a husband. Amelia, on the other hand, since dropping out of university, had done nothing but work. A series of idiotic, poorly paying and increasingly frustrating gigs. There was no such thing as full-time work for someone like her. Perhaps if she'd stuck with her studies, it might have been different, but when her mother got sick, she had to drop out and become her caretaker. And afterward, when her mother passed away, it wasn't like she could get her scholarship back.

"I do almost anything," Amelia said with a shrug. "Perhaps something in your husband's office?"

"There's nothing there," Fernanda said, too quickly.

There was likely *something* reserved for Fernanda's intimate friends. Amelia had once counted herself amongst those 'excellent' people. When they'd been in school together, Amelia had written a few term papers for Fernanda and that had made her useful. She'd also dated Elías Bertoliat, which had increased her standing amongst their cohort. That had gone to hell. He'd ghosted her, about two months after she'd dropped out of school, and returned to Monterrey.

Amelia was more devalued than the Mexican peso.

She looked at the bread basket, not wishing to lay her eyes on her so-called friend. She really didn't want to ask for money (it made her feel like shit), but of course that was the one reason why she was sitting at the restaurant.

"Anastasia Brito might be looking for someone like you," Fernanda said, breaking the uncomfortable silence that had descended between them.

Amelia frowned. Anastasia had gone to the same university, but she'd been an art student while Amelia dallied in land-and-food systems, looking forward to a career as an urban farmer.

"Why?" she asked.

"She's going through a phase. She has an art show in a couple of weeks. The theme is 'meat,' but after that, she said she's going to focus on plants and she'll be needing genetically modified ones. It might be your thing."

It was, indeed. After her chances at university soured up, Amelia had taken a few short-term courses in plant modification at a small-fry school. All she'd been able to do with that was get a gig at an illegal marijuana operation. Non-sanctioned, highly modified marijuana plants. It paid on time, but Amelia chickened out after a raid. You couldn't fly to Mars if your police certificate wasn't clean. She didn't want to risk it.

Her friend Pili told Amelia she was an idiot. Pili had been snared in raids four or five times. All she did was pay the fine.

But then, Pili did all kinds of crazy things. She sold her blood to old farts who paid for expensive transfusions, thinking the plasma could rejuvenate them.

"Could be. Do you have her number?" Amelia asked.

"She's in a great-super-cool women's temazcal retreat right now in Peru. All-natural, no contact with the outside world. Just meditation. But she will be back for the art show. You should just show up. I know someone at the gallery. They can put you on the list."

"The temazcal is Nahua. What's she doing in Peru?"

"I don't know, Amelia," Fernanda said, sounding annoyed. Amelia's geographical objections were clearly pointless. She supposed people organized whatever retreats rich fuckers could afford. Tibetan samatha in Brazil, Santería ceremonies in Dublin. Who cared?

"All right, put me on the list," Amelia said.

Fernanda seemed very pleased with herself and paid for the lunch after all. Amelia assumed she considered this her act of charity for the year. For her part, she felt stupidly proud for not mentioning anything about a loan, although she was going to have to figure something out soon.

Amelia picked her nieces up from school and, after ensuring they ate the food she had cooked, she made a quick escape from the apartment as soon as Marta arrived. This was Amelia's strategy: to spend as little time as possible in the apartment when her sister was around. Marta made a room shrink in size and Amelia's room already felt the size of a desk drawer.

Amelia hated sleeping in the same room she'd once shared with Marta, who'd moved to the master bedroom their mother had occupied. Each night, she looked at the walls she had looked at since she was a child. Stray stickers glued to her bed years before remained along the headboard. In a corner, there were smudged markings she'd made with crayons.

Not that it was an unusual set-up. Mexican youths, especially women, tended to live at home with their parents. These days, with the way the economy was going, even the most cosmopolitan people clustered together for long periods of time. At 25, Amelia didn't raise any eyebrows amongst her peers, but she still hated her living situation. Perhaps if they'd had a bigger apartment, it wouldn't be so annoying, but the apartment was small, the building they inhabited in disrepair: a government-funded unit, modern at one point when a president had been trying to score popularity points in that sector of the city. They were in one of four identical towers, built in a Brutalist style with the emphasis on the brute. An interior courtyard joined them together. Bored teens liked to gather there, while others held court in the lobby.

She loathed the whole complex and fled it every day. Her hours were spent navigating through several coffee shops. There was an art to this. The franchises used kiosks to sell coffee and tasteless bread wrapped in plastic. You pushed a button and out came your food. These were terrible places for sitting down for long periods of time. Since everything was automated, the job of the one or two idiots on staff was to wipe the tables clean, and to get people in and out as quick as possible. They enforced the maximum one-hour-for-customers rule with militaristic abandon.

Amelia hopped between two spots, three blocks from each other. One was a cafe and the other a crêperie. They were

on a decent street, meaning they both had an armed guard
standing at the door. But who didn't? Any Sanborns or Vips
had at least one and similar cafes employed at least a part-time
one for the busy times of the day. The guards kept the rabble
out. Otherwise, the patrons would have been shooing away
people offering to recharge cell phones by hooking them to
a tiny generator, or shifty strangers who would top up phone
cards for cheaper than the legit telecomm providers. Any other
number of peddlers of services and products could also slip in,
to the annoyance of licenciados in their suits and ties, trendy
youths in designer huipiles, and mothers leaning against their
deluxe, ultra-light strollers.

Amelia walked into the coffee shop, ordered a black
coffee — cheapest thing on the menu — and, with the day's
Wi-Fi code in hand, logged on to the Internet and began
reading. First, the news about Mars, then botany items. She
drifted haphazardly after that. Anything from celebrity news
to studying English or Mandarin. Those were the predominant
languages on Mars, German a distant third. After an
enthusiastic six months trying to grasp German, though, she'd
given up on it. Much of the same happened with Mandarin.
English she spoke well enough, as did any Mexican kid who'd
gone to a good school.

She'd also given up on a job search. Once she had updated
her CV, she had taken new headshots to go with it. Amelia,
black hair pulled back, looking like a docile employee. But with
her schooling interrupted, what should have been an impressive
degree from a nice university was just bullshit. And every time

she looked at the CV, it irritated her to see herself reduced to a pile of mediocrity:

Age: 25

Marital status: Unmarried

Current job: Freelancer

Freelancer. Euphemism for *unemployed.* Because her gigs didn't count. You couldn't put "professional friend" on a CV, any more than you could "professional cuddler." God knew there were people who did that gig, too, hiring themselves out to embrace people. She remembered seeing an ad for that explaining "99 percent of clients are male." Fuck, no.

Freelancer, then. Ex-university student, ex-someone. Her job applications disappeared into another dimension, swallowed by the computer until she simply stopped trying. She lived off gigs, first the marijuana operation, then odd jobs; for the past two years, the Friendrr bookings had constituted her sole income.

Freelancer. Fuck-up.

No more CV. Amelia focused on Mars, played video games on her cell, drew geometrical shapes on the napkins, then clovers for luck, and stars out of habit. When she knew she'd spent too much time at the coffee shop, she switched to the crêperie, where she repeated the process: black coffee, another couple of hours lost in mundane tasks.

When she was done, she took the subway back home.

It was always the same.

That night, a woman boarded Amelia's train and began asking people for a few tajaderos. The most popular cryptocurrency folks used since the peso was a piece of shit, jumping up and down in value faster than an addict dancing the jitterbug. You could tap a phone against another and transfer tajaderos from an account. A few people did just that, but even if the lady was old and rather pitiful, Amelia couldn't spare a dirty peso.

To be frank, just a couple of bad turns and Amelia would be begging in the subway right next to the old woman.

The doors of the car opened and Amelia darted out. On the walls of the concourse, there were floor-to-ceiling video displays. A blonde woman danced in them. RADIOACTIVE FLESH, she mouthed, the letters superimposed over her image. A NEW COLLECTION. A tattoo artist sat by one of these video panels. He was there every few days, tattooing sound waves onto people's arms. A snippet of your favorite song inked onto your flesh. With the swipe of a scanner, the melody would play. At first, she couldn't believe he lugged his equipment like that around the city, not because it was cumbersome, but because she expected someone might try to steal it. But the man was quite massive and his toothless grin was a warning.

"Hey, I'll give you a discount," the man told her, but she shook her head, as was her custom.

Amelia took the eastern exit, which was rarely frequented by the gangs. She was in luck; they were nowhere to be seen. Now there was a choice to make. Either follow the shortest route, which meant walking through the courtyard and encountering the young louts who would be drinking there, or take the long way around the perimeter of the complex.

Amelia picked the short way. In the center of the courtyard, there was a dry fountain, filled with rubbish. All around lounged teenagers from the buildings. They were not gang members, just professional loafers who specialized in playing loud music and yelling a choice obscenity or two at any girl who walked by.

Although the kids had nothing to offer except, perhaps, cigarettes and a bottle of cheap booze, when Amelia had been a teenager, she'd peered curiously at them. They seemed to be having a good time. Her mother, however, forbade any contact with the teenagers from the housing unit. Mother emphasized how Amelia was meant for bigger and better things. Marta was a lost cause. She'd gotten herself pregnant her last year in high school and married a man who ran off after a handful of years. It didn't matter. Marta possessed no great intellectual gifts, anyway. She'd flunked a grade and barely finished her high school through online courses. Amelia, however, was a straight-A student. She couldn't waste her time crushing beer cans with *those* kids.

Amelia believed this narrative. When her mother learned she was going out with a good boy from the university, she was ecstatic. Elías Bertoliat, with his pale skin and light eyes, and his fancy car, seemed like a prince from a fairy tale. Every time Amelia floated the idea of Mars, her mother immediately told her Mars was unlikely and she should focus on marrying Elías. After he broke up with Amelia, her mother insisted they'd get back together.

Glancing at the boys kicking around a beer can and laughing, Amelia wondered if she wouldn't have been better off partying with them when she had the chance. If she was destined to be a loser, she could at least have been a loser who had fun, fucked lots of people, enjoyed her youth while it lasted.

She looked at the girls sitting chatting near the fountain, in stockings and shorts, heavy chains dangling against their breasts, their nails long, the makeup plentiful. Then one of the boys hollered and another followed.

"Were you going? I've got something for you, baby."

Laughter. Amelia looked ahead. There was no point in acknowledging their displays. The faint fantasy that she might have once enjoyed spending her time with them vanished.

They called the days on Mars "sol." 24 hours, 39 minutes, and 35.244 second adding up to a sol. Three percent shorter than a day on Earth. She reminded herself of this. It was important to keep her focus on what mattered, on the facts. They could scream, "Show me your pussy!" and ask her to give them a blowjob, but she did not listen.

When she reached her building, she climbed the five flights of stairs up to her apartment — the elevator was perpetually busted. A dog padded down the long hallway, which led to her apartment. Many tenants had pets and some let them roam wild, as if the building were a park. The animals defecated on the stairs, but they also kept the indigents away. The teens who held court downstairs also provided a measure of safety.

Amelia paused before her door, fished out her keys from her purse, and stood still. She could hear dialogue from the TV, muffled, but loud enough she could make out a few words. Amelia walked in.

"Let's see what's behind Door Number One!" the TV announcer yelled. Clapping ensued.

MARS, SCENE 1

It's nothing but sand dunes. Dry, barren, quiet. When she bends down and picks up a handful of sun-baked soil, and wipes her hand against her pale dress, it leaves a dark, rusty streak.

There is air here. This is Mars but the Mars of EXT. MARS SURFACE — DAY. And she is a SPACE EXPLORER, a young woman in a white dress now streaked red.

SPACE EXPLORER has no lines of dialogue, not yet. The camera hovers over her shoulder, over tendrils of dark hair, which shift with the wind.

There is even wind, in EXT. MARS SURFACE. And the dress is far too impractical for any true 'space exploration.' It reaches her ankle, shows off her arms, although no cleavage. Instead, a demure collar that reaches the chin indicates SPACE EXPLORER is a good girl. The white might have clued you in, but it never hurts to place the proper signifiers.

PRIME MERIDIAN

SPACE EXPLORER looks over her shoulder and sees a figure coming toward her, glinting under the sunlight.

Hold that shot, hold that moment, as the HERO steps into the frame.

ㅌ

Amelia avoided her sister for three days, but on the fourth, Marta caught her before she could slip out of the apartment, cornering her by the refrigerator, which was covered with drawings made by the youngest girl. Amelia's niece had a good imagination: The sky was never blue in Mexico City.

"The rent is due," Marta said. "And you still owe me that money."

Two months before, Amelia had bought a pretty new dress. It wasn't a bargain, but it seemed she was getting another steady Friendrr client. Every week, like the arrangement with Lucía. Four hours. She bought the dress because she thought she deserved it. She hadn't bought anything for herself in forever and she would be able to afford it now. Then that client canceled a booking, and another, and Amelia had to pay for the layaway or lose all the money she'd ponied up. So, she asked Marta for enough to make the final payment.

"I have the rent money, not the rest. Things are slow right now," Amelia said. "I'm sure bookings will improve as we roll into December."

"Oh, for God's sake," Marta said, sending a magnet in the shape of a watermelon slice flying into the air as she slapped her hand against the refrigerator's door. "You need to get a real job that pays on time."

"There are no real jobs," Amelia replied.

"Then what do I do every day?"

Marta was an end-of-life planner, helping arrange elaborate funerals, memorials and euthanasia packages. And yes, it was a job, but guess what? She only had it because she sucked good dick for the boss, a smarmy little man who had made a pass at Amelia the year before, when Marta took her to an office party. He had suggested a threesome with the sisters and when Amelia complained to Marta about her vomit-inducing creep of a part-time boyfriend/supervisor, Marta had the gall to tell Amelia she shouldn't have worn such a tight skirt.

"You need to look into the private security company I told you about," Marta said. "They are always hiring."

"Do I look like I can shoot a rifle?"

"Fuck it, Amelia, it's just standing on your feet for a few hours holding the gun, not shooting it. Surely, even you can manage that?"

Amelia swallowed a mouthful of rage. She couldn't afford a place on her own and so, she swallowed it, bile and resentment making her want to spit.

The phone rang. She almost didn't hear it because the kids had the television on so loud and the kitchen was smack next to the living room/dining room area. It was Miguel, her broker. Friendrr called him that: Junior Social Appointment Broker. Amelia thought it was a weird, long title.

"Hey Amelia, now, how are you doing today?" Miguel asked in that oddly chirpy tone he employed. She'd never met him in person, but Miguel always sounded like he was smiling and his profile featured multiple shots of him grinning at different locations. The beach, a concert, an assortment of restaurants.

Miguel was an extreme positive thinker. He had told her he liked to read self-help books. He also took a lot of online courses. In the beginning, they'd bonded a bit over this, since Amelia was still trying to learn German. As the months dragged by, they both grew disenchanted.

Amelia simply wasn't the kind of girl who could secure many clients. There were some people who were booked solid for gigs, but most of them were very good-looking. She'd heard one young woman got booked exclusively to pose for photos. The kind of 'candid' shots where friends gathered for a social event. Nothing candid in them. Then there were others who did all right with weddings and funerals. Both of these required an ability to cry.

Amelia wasn't a crybaby and she wasn't gorgeous. Her biggest issue, though, was that she simply did not inspire friendly feelings. People did not want to meet her and if they did, they did not want to meet her again. Whatever warmth or spark is required to inspire a desire for human interaction was lacking in her. She wasn't compelling.

Miguel had told her she needed better photos, more keywords. They tried a bunch of things, but it didn't work. Miguel, who had been excited because her science background gave her a certain versatility — some of the folks on Friendrr could hardly spell 'cat,' the glorious, underfunded public education system at play — grew underwhelmed.

Miguel hadn't phoned her in weeks and Amelia feared he was getting ready to drop her from Friendrr. She was probably driving his stats down.

"I'm good," she said, turning her back to her sister, grateful for the interruption. She headed to the room and locked the door. "What's up?"

"I have a booking for you, you have a new client. That's what's up. The only thing is, it's short notice: tonight at nine."

"I'm not doing anything tonight."

"Good. It's in New Polanco. I'm sending you the address."

"Any special items?"

"No," Miguel said. "He wants to have dinner."

Most clients wanted ordinary things, like watching movies, as Lucía had asked, or walking together. Now and then, an oddity emerged. There had been a man who asked that she wear white gloves and sit perfectly still for a whole hour. But most baffling had been the time a client hired her to pretend she was someone else. Amelia bore a vague resemblance to an old lady's favorite daughter, who had passed away many years before. Or perhaps Amelia bore no resemblance; perhaps any young woman would do. The old woman wept when she saw her, confessing a small litany of sins. They had parted on bad terms, then the daughter died.

Amelia was unnerved by the experience. She wondered if this was the first time a young woman had been brought to meet the old woman. She wondered if other people had worn the green sweater she had been asked to wear. Had it belonged to the dead girl, or was it merely a similar sweater? Were there many girls dressed in green sweaters, each one ushered into the room on a different day of the week?

Worst of all, while the old woman gripped Amelia's hand and swore she'd never leave her alone again, Amelia raised her head and caught sight of the person who had hired her for this gig. It was the old woman's surviving daughter. Her eyes were hard and distant.

Amelia wondered what it must be like for her, to accompany these look-alikes to her mother's bedroom, to have them sit next to her, to hold the woman's hand. What did she feel, being the daughter the old woman did not want? The one who was superfluous?

Perhaps she might have obtained more bookings at that house, but Amelia refused to go back and even though Miguel said she was being stupid — there was talk about terms of agreement, clauses — she refused. Miguel let it go. For once.

*

The tower where the client lived was a thin, white, luxurious needle, the kind the ads assured would-be buyers was not only 'modern,' but 'super modern.' Many warehouses had been scrapped to make way for these monstrous buildings. The old housing units that remained — homes of the descendants of factory workers, of lower-class citizens who toiled assembling cars and bought little plots to build their homes —

existed under the shadow of behemoths. Since the expensive buildings required abundant water and electricity, the poor residents in the area had to do without. The big buildings had priority over all the resources. There were also a few fancy buildings that had halted construction when the latest housing bubble popped. They remained half-finished, like gaping, filthy teeth spread across several gigantic lots. Indigents now made their homes there, living in structures without windows, while three blocks away, women were wrapped in tepezcohuite at the spa, experiencing the trendiest traditional plant remedy around the city.

Amelia walked into the lobby of the white building. A concierge and a guard with a submachine gun both stood behind a glistening desk. The concierge smiled. The guard did not acknowledge her in any way.

"I'm expected. Number 1201," Amelia said. The client had not given a name, although that was not unusual.

"Yes, you are," the concierge said, the smile the same, pleasant without being exactly warm. The concierge walked Amelia to the elevator and swiped a card so she could board it.

When she reached the door to 1201, Amelia saw it had been left unlocked and she walked in. The apartment was open concept. The portion constituting the living room area was dominated by a shaggy rug and a modular, low-slung sofa in tasteful gray with an integrated side table. Floor-to-ceiling windows allowed one to observe the cityscape.

She could see the kitchen, but there was a gray sliding door to the right. She assumed a bedroom and bathroom lay in that direction.

"Hey, I'm here," Amelia said. "Hello?"

The gray door opened and there stood Elías Bertoliat. For a minute, she thought it was merely a man who *resembled* Elías. Who just happened to have Elías' mouth, his nose, his green eyes. Because it didn't sound feasible that she had just walked into the apartment of her ex-boyfriend.

"You've got to be kidding me," she said at last. "You booked me?"

He raised his hands, as if to pacify her.

"Amelia, this is going to sound nuts, but if you'll let me explain —" and his voice was not quite the same. The years had given it more weight, a deeper resonance, but there was still the vague choppiness of the words, as if he'd rehearsed for a long time, attempting to rid himself of his Northern accent, and almost managed it.

"It doesn't sound nuts. It *is*," she said clutching her cell phone and pointing it at him. "Are you stalking me?"

"No! I saw your profile on Friendrr by chance. I don't have your contact info, or I would have gotten a hold of you some other way. I just saw it and I thought I'd talk to you."

Just like that, so easy. And yet, it sounded entirely like him: careless, swift. To see her and decide to find her, like he had decided once, on the spur of the moment, that they ought to go to Monterrey for a concert. Fly in and fly out.

"Why?" she asked. "You were a dick to me."

"I know."

"You don't date someone for two years and then take off like that. Not even a fucking text message, a phone call."

She didn't care if ghosting was fashionable, or her generation simply didn't care for long-term relationships, or whatever half-baked pop psychology article explained this shit.

He approached her, but Amelia moved away from him, ensuring the sofa was between them, that it served as a demarcation line. Sinus Meridiani in the middle of the living room.

"My dad pulled me from university. He didn't like all my talk about going to Mars and he forced me to go back home," he said.

"And he forced you to ghost me."

"I didn't know what to say. I was a kid," he protested.

"We were in university, not kindergarten."

He managed to look betrayed despite the fact she should have owned all the outrage in this meeting. He had looked, when they'd met, rather boyish. Little boy lost. This had been an interesting change from the loud, grossly wealthy 'juniors' who populated the university and the festive, catcalling youths in the center of her housing complex. And he had an interest in photography, which revealed a sensitive soul. It, in turn, prompted Amelia to forgive whatever mistakes he made, since she was a misguided romantic in search of a Prince Charming.

He still had that boyishness, in the eyes if not the face.

"What do you want?" she asked.

"I was on Friendrr for the same reason other people are. I wanted to talk to someone. I thought I'd talk to you. Maybe apologize. Amelia, let me buy you dinner."

To be fair, she considered it and just as quickly, she decided, *Fuck, no.*

"You booked me for two hours," she said, holding the phone tight, holding it up, so he could look at the timer she'd just switched on. "But I am not having dinner with you. In fact, I'm going to lock myself in your room and I'm going to take a nap. A long nap."

She closed the sliding door behind her and walked down a wide hallway, which led straight into said room. She promptly locked the door, as she'd promised. The bed was large, no narrow, lumpy mattress, springs digging into her back. She turned her head and stared at the curtains. She didn't sleep, not a wink, and he didn't attempt to coax her out of there. When the two hours had elapsed, Amelia walked back into the living room.

"At Friendrr, your satisfaction is of the utmost importance to us. I hope you will consider us again for all your social needs," she said.

Elías was sitting on the sofa. When she spoke, he turned his head, staring at her. He had enjoyed taking pictures, but did not often have his own taken. Yet, she had snapped a rare shot of him with his own camera. He'd had the same expression in that shot: remote, somewhat flimsy, as if he were afraid the raw camera lens might reveal a hidden blemish.

Three months after he'd dumped her, Amelia had deleted that photo from her computer, erasing him from her hard drive and her life after finally clueing in to the fact that he was never coming back. Now she walked out and walked downstairs, not bothering to wait for the elevator.

I don't know why you're on Mars, Carl Sagan once said. Amelia had committed his speech to memory, but she couldn't remember it now, although she'd played it back to Elías, for Elías. Elías, brushing the hair away from her face as she pressed a key on the laptop and the astronomer's voice came out loud and clear. Which was maybe why she couldn't, wouldn't remember it.

4

Amelia had been tired, busy, upset, but the movie playing was too terrible to remember her worries. Too ridiculous. A man in an ape suit jumped around, chasing a young woman, and Lucía chuckled. Amelia, noticing this, chuckled, too. They both glanced at each other. Then they erupted in synchronized laughter. The ape-man stumbled, pointed a raygun at the screen, and they both laughed even more.

Afterward, a servant refilled their glasses with mineral water. Lucía wore a yellow turban, embroidered with flowers.

"Not my finest performance, I suppose," Lucía said, smiling. "In my defense, the ape costume was terrible. It smelled like rotten eggs for some reason. God knows where they got it from."

"That doesn't sound very glamorous."

Amelia did not ask questions, she simply listened, but for once, Lucía was offering conversation. Months of starchiness and at last, the old woman had seemed to warm up to her.

Perhaps this boded well. It would certainly be nice if she could book more hours. Especially considering that damned fiasco with Elías. Would he attempt to book her again? Amelia had asked herself that question a dozen times already. Each time, she thought she needed to phone Miguel, tell him this was her damned ex-boyfriend trying to book her, but she felt too embarrassed.

"It wasn't," the older woman said. "The glamor was in the 40s and 50s. I was born too late. The movie industry in Mexico was eroding by the time the 60s rolled around. We made terrible movies, cheap flicks. Go-go dancers and wrestlers and monsters. I might have done a Viking movie if Nahum had gotten the funding for that, but he was flying low and Armand Elba wasn't doing much better, either. Can you imagine? Viking women in Mexico."

"Nahum?"

"Nahum Landmann. The director. They billed him as Eduard Landmann. Armando Elba was the scriptwriter. They worked on three films before Nahum went to Chile. The first one did well enough, a Western. And then they shot the Mars movie: *Conqueror Women of Mars*. Then came that stupid ape movie and the Viking project floundered. Nahum couldn't get any money and Elba flew back to Europe. Maybe it was for the best."

"Why?"

"The movies were supposed to be completely different. Well, maybe not the Western. That one turned out close to the original concept. But Nahum saw the Mars movie as a surrealist project. The original title was *Adelita of Mars*. Can you picture that?"

Amelia could not, although that explained the strange costume choices and even certain shots, which had seemed oddly out of place.

"Women wearing cartridge belts like during the Revolution, a guy dressed like a futuristic Pancho Villa. It was more Luis Buñuel and *Simon of the Desert* than a B movie. A long prologue, nearly half an hour of it. But then the producers asked for changes. Nahum also demanded changes, Elba kept rewriting and then Nahum rewrote the rewrites. I had new pages every morning. I didn't know how to say my lines. I didn't know the ending."

"Did they make any other movies?"

"Elba wrote erotic science fiction. Paperbacks, I don't remember in what language. Was it in French or German?" the old woman wondered. "Nahum didn't do any other movies. He didn't do anything at all, although he sent me a few sketches from Chile. He had another idea: robot women!"

Lucía smiled broadly and then her painted eyebrows knitted in a frown.

"And then it was '73 in Chile and the Coup," she muttered.

Lucía sipped her mineral water in silence, her lipstick leaving a red imprint on the plastic straw. She glanced at Amelia, as if sizing her up.

"Come. Let me show you something," the old woman said.

Amelia followed her. She had only been inside the one room in the house where they watched the movies. Lucía took her to her office. There were tall bookcases, a rustic pine desk with painted sunflowers. Several framed posters served as decoration. Lucía stood before one of them.

"*Conqueror Women of Mars*," she said. "The first poster. They had it redone. Cristina Garza said, since she was the better-known actress, she should be on the poster. They made a terrible poster to promote the film, but this was a good concept. It was better."

The poster showed a woman in white, cartridge belts crisscrossing her back. There was one brief scene in the movie where Lucía was dressed like that. The ground beneath the woman's feet was red and the sky was also red, a cloud of dust. She was looking over her shoulder. The colors were saturated and the font was all-caps, dramatic. But there was an element of gracefulness in the woman's pose that elevated this from shlock to sheer beauty.

"I like it," Amelia said.

"Then look at this one," Lucía said, pointing at another poster. "To raise money for the Viking project, Nahum commissioned an artist to paint this. It was a lost-world story but with a science fiction twist. It was set in the future, after an atomic war has left most of the world uninhabited and giant lizards roam the desert."

"Where did the Vikings come into that?" Amelia said, puzzled, staring at this other poster, which showed a young Lucía in a fur bikini, clutching the arm of a handsome man who wore an incongruous Viking hat. Behind them, two dinosaurs were engaged in a vicious fight.

"I don't know. But you have to remember Raquel Welch had made a lot of money in *One Million Years B.C.* and this was just a few years after that. I suppose any concept was a good concept if they could get half a dozen pretty girls into furry bathing suits."

"So, why couldn't the director raise the money for it, then?"

"Same problem as always. Nahum had all these strange ideas he wanted to incorporate into the movie and he kept fighting with Elba. Nahum could have been Alejandro Jodorowsky, but things didn't quite go that way and besides, there already was *one* Jewish Latin-American director. In fact, I'm pretty sure Nahum went to Chile because he was so pissed off at Jodorowsky. If Jodorowsky had gone from Chile to Mexico, then Nahum was going from Mexico to Chile."

"If he had a cast ready, he must have gotten pretty far," Amelia mused, looking at the names on the poster.

"He had all the main parts figured out. Rodrigo Tinto was going to be the Hero, same as in *Mars*. He looked great on camera, which is the best I can say of him."

"You did not like him?" Amelia asked, a little surprised. They seemed to have good chemistry in the movie she'd watched. Then again, it was a film with rayguns and space pirates, nothing but make-believe.

"He had bad breath and a temper."

"What about the director? Was he likeable?"

"No," Lucía said. Her smile was dismissive but not toward Amelia. She was thinking back to her acting days.

"Also had a temper?"

"No. Darling, some people are not meant to be liked," Lucía said, with elegant simplicity.

Amelia did not know what that meant. Perhaps, judging by her lack of gigs on Friendrr, Amelia was one of those persons who were not meant to be liked. And judging by the film director's lack of success, they might share more than that single quality.

Lucía showed Amelia a couple of more posters before they said goodbye. In the subway concourse, she saw an ad for a virtual assistant, a dancing, singing, 3D hologram: a teenage avatar in a skimpy French maid's outfit who would call you "Master" and wake you up in the morning with a song.

Her phone, tucked inside her jacket, rang. The specific ringtone she knew. She had a booking.

She pressed a hand against the cell phone and resisted the impulse to check her messages. Finally, in the stairway to her building, Amelia took out the phone and looked at the screen. It was a booking with Elías, just as she'd suspected. She could press the green button and accept it, or click on the big red "no" button and discard it. But Miguel would ring her up and ask for an explanation. He was zealous about this stuff. Each rejected booking was a lost commission.

Amelia's index finger hovered over the green button. Accepting was easier than speaking to Miguel. She could spend another two hours locked in Elías' room. After all, he had given her a good rating. Five out of five stars. She remembered when she used to agonize over each rating she obtained, wondering why people hadn't liked her enough. Three stars, two. Even when it was four, she wondered. She had wanted to be like the popular ones, the ones who got bookings every day. If she could up her ratings by a quarter of a point… and there was a bonus for customer satisfaction. It did not amount to anything, not ever.

There was a sour note in her. It drove people away. And Jesus Christ, if she could be more cheerful, nicer, friendlier, she would be, but it was no use.

Green. It didn't matter. Booking confirmed.

✶

The view from Elías's apartment at night rendered the city strange. It turned it into an entirely different city. In the distance, a large billboard flickered red, enticing people to 'Visit Mars.' You could emigrate now; see more information online.

The words 'Visit Mars' alternated with the image of a girl in a white spacesuit, holding a helmet under her arm, looking up at the sky. Her face confident. That girl knew things. That girl knew people. That girl was not Amelia, because Amelia was no one.

Elías emerged from the kitchen and handed her a glass of white wine. Amelia continued staring out the tall windows.

"What are you looking at?" he asked.

"That billboard," she said. The glow of the sign was mesmerizing.

"Mars. It's always Mars," he said, raising his own glass of wine to his lips.

"You used to be interested in it."

"I still am. But things are different now. I just... I thought you'd changed your mind."

He had definitely changed *his* mind. There were no photos in the apartment. His old place was small. Photos on the walls, antique cameras on the shelves, hand-painted stars on the ceiling (those had been her notion). An attempt at bohemian living. It had all been scrubbed clean, just like his face, the whole look of him.

"Never."

"New Panyu, is that still the idea?" he asked.

Amelia nodded. They had weighed all three options. New Panyu seemed the best bet, the largest settlement. They'd quizzed each other in Mandarin. Yī shēng yī shì, whispered against the curve of her neck. Funny how 'I love you' never sounded the same in different languages. It lost or gained power. In English, it sounded so plain. In Spanish, it became a promise.

"It mustn't be easy," he said. He looked like he was sorry for her. It irritated Amelia.

"Haven't you heard? The problem with our generation is we don't have enough life goals," Amelia replied tersely. "No real challenges."

"My assistant said they are capping Class B applications."

"Is it a virtual assistant? I say 'she' because it turns out men like to interact with female avatars," Amelia told him. She thought about the French maid hologram bending over to show her underwear, but surely he could afford real people. He was on Friendrr. Maybe in the mornings, a chick came to play dictation with him, wearing glasses and holding a clipboard.

"No."

"Do you want me to keep talking to you, or do you want me to be quiet? You need to give me parameters of interaction," she said.

"Please don't talk like that."

"You clicked on an app and ordered me like you order Chinese takeout, so don't be offended if I ask if you'd like chopsticks."

He stared at her and she gave him a faint smile, but it wasn't real. It was the cheap, placid imitation she ironed and took out for clients.

"I'm fine with silence. I just want to have a few drinks. I don't like drinking alone," he said coolly.

She finished her wine. He refilled the glass. They moved away from the window, sat on different ends of the couch. They drank and she watched him, Elías in profile. She might have taken out her cell phone and played a game, but she wanted him to be uncomfortable, to ask her to look away. He did not and eventually, Amelia relaxed her body and took off her shoes, staring at the ceiling, instead. The wine had a hint of citrus. It went to her head quickly. She did not drink too often these days, not when she was paying, and when she did, it was the cheap, watered stuff.

She enjoyed the feeling that came with the alcohol, the indifference as she lay on his couch and threw her head back. She thought of Mars, the Mars in Lucía's movie, tinted in black-and-white, and she shielded her eyes with the back of her hand. She drank more. Time had slowed down in the silence of the room.

Finally, the cell phone beeped and she rose, pressing the heel of her hand against her forehead.

"Well," she said, standing in front of him and showing him the phone, "it's over."

"I can add an extra hour," he said. "Let me find my phone."

He looked panicked as he patted his shirt. He accidentally knocked over the glass of wine, which had been resting on the arm of the couch. The wine splattered over the expensive rug. Amelia chuckled, his distress delighting her. But then he looked hurt and she felt somewhat bad, for a heartbeat.

Amelia sat on his lap, straddling him, her hands resting on his shoulders.

"What's so terrible about being alone?" she asked.

She was being deliberately cruel, teasing him. She disliked it when she sank to such depths, but Amelia was angry, with a quiet sort of anger. She might hurt him now and it would please her.

Elías did not move. He had flailed like a fish out of water a few seconds before as he attempted to find his phone, but now he was perfectly still, staring at her.

"I hate it and you know it."

"Can't you hire someone to scare the monster who lives under the bed?"

"Amelia," he said, sadly.

She chuckled. "Aren't we pathetic?" she whispered.

When he tried to kiss her, she wouldn't let him. An arbitrary line but one she had to trace. Fucking was fine. Amelia hadn't fucked in forever. She couldn't bring people to her shared room and the guys she stumbled into were in as much of a fix as she was. She didn't want anyone, anyway. It was a struggle to exchange semi-polite words, to pretend she was interested in what came out of a stranger's mouth. *Oh, yes, that's great how you're going to take a coding boot camp and you'll have a job in six weeks or less, except no one is hiring, you idiot.* Or, *That's interesting that you are working as a pimp on the side, but no thanks, buddy, I'm not joining your troupe or whatever the hell it's called these days.*

Who cared what she said to Elías? What she did with him? Who cared at this point? She drew her line and he drew his, which seemed to be the ridiculous notion that they should fuck on the bed. Perhaps he objected to the soiling of the couch.

By the time Amelia zipped up her jeans and started pulling on her shoes, it was too late to take the bus. She had to call a car. She fiddled with the cell phone.

"Will you give me your number?" Elías asked. "I don't want to keep using this Friendrr thing to find you."

"I should tell you to make me an offer," she replied.

He looked at her, offended, but then his gaze softened. She feared perhaps he might bark an amount after all. The thought that he might take her seriously, or that she had said it in anything but mockery, made Amelia reach for her purse. She found a stray piece of paper and scribbled the number.

"Bye," she told him and headed downstairs.

MARS, SCENE 2

INT. MARS BASE — NIGHT

SPACE EXPLORER sits next to the bed where THE HERO lies. He is injured. His ship crashed near her father's lab. He dragged himself from the wreckage. She cleans and bandages his wounds. SPACE EXPLORER is not truly a space explorer. The script has been rewritten and she is now ROMANTIC INTEREST, but for the sake of expediency, we will continue to call her SPACE EXPLORER. THE HERO shall remain THE HERO.

SPACE EXPLORER tenderly speaks to THE HERO. This is love at first sight, for both of them. THE HERO tells SPACE EXPLORER how he's come to warn and protect the outpost from a marauding band of SPACE PIRATES. But SPACE EXPLORER's father thinks something else may be afoot. He is a dedicated scientist working on a top secret project and fears THE HERO may be a spy from an evil nation sent to steal his work.

Despite only knowing THE HERO for five minutes, SPACE EXPLORER defends the stranger. Later, during an interlude inside the 'futuristic' outpost, which is a building shaped like an egg, THE HERO kisses SPACE EXPLORER.

Cue swelling music with plenty of violins. Fade to modest black.

5

The Zócalo was being transformed into a cheesy winter wonderland, complete with an ice skating rink. The city's mayor trotted the rink out each year to please the crowds: free skating, fake snow falling from the sky, a giant Coca-Cola-sponsored tree in the background. It wasn't bread-and-circuses, anymore. Now it was icicles and festive music.

This spectacle meant a lot of people wanting to make a buck were ready for action. Teenagers in ratty "snowman" costumes offering to pose for a photo, peddlers selling soda pop to people waiting in line, and thieves eager to steal purses.

Pili was also downtown. Like anyone their age, Pili had no permanent job, cycling between gigs. Working at the marijuana grow-op, checking ATMs in small businesses to make sure no one was skimming them, selling spare computer parts Christmas season this year found her servicing the machines at a virtual reality arcade.

"They're probably going to shut them down in a few months," Pili said. "All that talk about virtual reality dissociation."

"Is that a real thing?" Amelia asked.

"Fuck if I know. But the Mayor needs to score points with the old farts, and if he can't combat prostitution and crime, this is the next best thing. Virtual reality addiction."

"It seems like it would be a lot of trouble to shut everyone down. There's a lot of arcades."

"It'll just go underground. Fuck it. It's slow today, ain't it? We should have gone to the Sanborns."

They were eating at the Bhagavad, which wasn't a restaurant proper but a weird joint run by a bunch of deluded eco-activists, open only at odd and irregular hours. You paid what you wanted and sat next to walls plastered with flyers warning people against the dangers of vat-meat. Amelia didn't care about veganism, Indian spirituality, or the fight against capitalist oppressors, but she did care about spending as little as possible on her meals. Not that there weren't affordable tacos near the subway, but like everyone joked, long gone were the days when they were at least made with dog. Nowadays, rat was the most likely source of protein. She did not fancy swallowing bubonic plague wrapped in a tortilla.

Unfortunately, the bohemian candor and community spirit of Bhagavad meant the service was terrible. They had spent half an hour waiting for the rice dish of the day, which would inevitably taste like shit watered in piss, but must have some kind of nutritional content, since it kept many a sorry ass like Amelia going.

"Do you have to be back by a certain time?" Amelia asked.

"Kind of."

"Sorry."

"It's okay. I'll grab a protein shake if it gets too late," Pili said, dismissing any issues with a wave of her hand.

Pili was always cool. Nothing ever seemed to faze her, whether it was the cops suddenly appearing and chasing away street vendors while she was trying to hawk computer parts, or the sight of a bloated, dead dog in the middle of the road blocking her path. Perhaps such self-confidence came from a secret, inner well, but Amelia suspected Pili's tremendous height had something to do it. Pili was strong, as well. She wore sleeveless shirts, which showed off her arms and her tattoos, and she smiled a lot.

"All right. But if it gets too late, just say the word."

"Nah, don't worry. Hey, you still need that money?"

"No, I had a gig," Amelia said, thinking of the two times she'd seen Elías.

"Friendrr, hu? Look, you can make a lot more at the blood clinic. The only requirement is that you have to be 27 or younger, no diseases, no addicts."

Amelia knew it was easy. That was what scared her. She was inching toward 27 and after that, what could she sell? What could she do when she wasn't even fit to be a blood bag? She didn't want to get hooked on that kind of money, but there didn't seem to be anything else beckoning her.

Giovanni Schiaparelli peered into his telescope and he thought he saw canals on Mars. Lowell imagined alien civilizations: "Framed in the blue of space, there floats before the observer's gaze a seeming miniature of his own Earth, yet changed by translation to the sky."

Mars, Amelia's Mars. Always Mars, in every stolen and quiet moment, as she folded a napkin and refolded it.

"You've got that face again, Amelia."

"What face?" Her fingers stilled on the napkin.

"Like you don't care I'm here."

"Of course I care."

"If you need the money, just ask. I can lend you the stuff. I know you'll pay me back."

"It's not the money."

Well, it wasn't only the money. Not that she was doing fine in terms of cash flow. It was Elías and she couldn't discuss him with Pili. It was Mars and there was no point in discussing that with anybody.

"I'm throwing a party Friday. You should come. It'll do you good," Pili suggested.

"I have to go to an art gallery. I'm trying to meet someone there about a gig," Amelia said.

"What time is that?"

"Eight."

"We'll be up late. Just stop by after your meeting."

"I don't know," Amelia said. She turned her head, staring at a neon pink flyer stuck on the wall that showed several politicians drawn in the shape of pigs, wearing ties and jackets. They were eating slops.

It was hard to believe that this metropolis, when viewed from Presidente Masaryk, was the place where Amelia lived, scrubbed clean, with a Ferrari dealership and luxurious shops. The city attempted to eliminate the grimy fingerprints that clung to the rest of the urban landscape. Private security kept a tight watch on beggars and indigents. There were trees here —

not plastic ones, either. Real bits of greenery, while elsewhere a sea of cement swallowed the soul.

She had ventured down Masaryk often when she was with Elías. His interest in photography led them there to inspect the art galleries that perched themselves near the wide avenue. The place where Anastasia had her opening was a new gallery. Amelia had never visited it with her ex-boyfriend.

She wore the nice gray dress, which had caused her so many headaches. It was classic, elegant and it paired perfectly with one of the few pairs of heels she owned. She'd slicked her hair back into a ponytail, put on eyeshadow, which she didn't bother with most mornings.

The theme of the exhibit was indeed, obviously, crassly "meat." There were hunks of beef hanging from the ceiling, cube-shaped meat that gently palpitated. Alive. Vat-meat, coerced into this shape. The head of a bull atop a pillar stared at Amelia. It smelled. Coppery, intense, the smell. It made Amelia wrinkle her nose. The other guests did not seem to mind the stench, long, glass flutes in their hands, laughter on their lips.

Amelia saw Anastasia Brito surrounded by a wide circle of admirers. She waited, trying to slip to her side, and found herself squeezed next to three people who were having an animated discussion about fish.

"Soon, the only thing left to eat is going to be jellyfish. It's the one animal thriving in the ocean," a man with a great, bald pate said.

"The indigenous people in — fuck it, I don't know where, some shit place in Asia — they are launching some sort of lawsuit," replied a young man.

"It's really sad," said a woman with cherry-red lips. "But what is anyone supposed to do about it?"

The young man stopped a waiter, grabbing a shrimp and popping it in his mouth. Amelia traced a vector toward Anastasia and correctly inserted herself at her elbow, catching her attention.

"Hi, Anastasia, it's good to see you again. This is all very interesting."

Anastasia smiled at Amelia, but Amelia could tell she did not remember her, that for a few seconds, she simply threw her a canned, indifferent smile before her eyes focused on her and the smile turned into an O of surprise

"Amelia. Why… it's been ages. What are you doing here?" she asked, and she looked like she'd discovered gum stuck under her shoe.

"Fernanda told me about the show and I decided to give it a look," Amelia said. She'd assumed Fernanda would mention she would be showing up, that something would have been indicated. She should not have expected such attention to detail.

"Well," Anastasia said. She said nothing else. The canned smile returned, brighter than before, but Anastasia's eyes scanned the room, as if she were looking for someone, anyone, to pull her out of this unwanted reunion.

Amelia dug in. She'd made the trip to the stupid gallery, after all. Marta was always chiding her about her lack of initiative. So, Amelia smiled back and tried to move the conversation in the required direction.

"Fernanda said you are putting together something new. Something about plants. She thought I might be able to help you with it."

"How?" Anastasia asked.

"I do have the studies in botany and I've gotten good at hacking genes. Here's my card," Amelia said, handing Anastasia the little plastic square with her contact information. She'd spent money getting this new card, money she didn't have, so she wouldn't hand out a number scribbled on a crumpled napkin. Anastasia held it with the tips of her fingers. Her nails were painted a molten gold. The tips of her eyelashes had been inked in gold to match the nails.

"No offense, Amelia, but what do you know about art?"

"A few things. Elías and I spent a lot of time around galleries and museums."

"That's great, but wasn't that such a long time ago?" she asked, and her words carried a hint of disgust.

The smile once more. The silence. Amelia remembered all the times Miguel had told her success was all about acquiring a positive attitude. She dearly wished to dial him and tell him he was an idiot. Instead, she bade Anastasia a quick goodbye and went in search of a car.

5

Pili lived in a rough area. It wasn't La Joya or Barrio Norte, but Santa María la Ribera kept getting more fucked-up each year. There were benefits to this, mainly that when Pili threw a party — even if the whole floor joined in, blasting music from each apartment — the neighbors upstairs couldn't do shit about it. If they called the cops, the cops were liable to show up, have a couple of beers, dance a cumbia, and depart.

Pili threw parties often and Amelia declined any invitations just as often. She had internalized her mother's directives: Study, work hard, don't drink, no boys. It was difficult to shake those manacles off. Whenever she did, Amelia felt guilty. But she didn't want to think about her conversation with Anastasia at the gallery — the fucking humiliation of it — and the music at Pili's apartment eviscerated coherent thoughts.

Amelia pushed into Pili's place, trying to find her friend amongst the dancers and the people resting on the couch, chatting, drinking, smoking. Finally, she spotted Pili in a corner, laughing her generous laughter.

"Amelia!" Pili said. "You came after all. And you look like a secretary or some shit like that."

Amelia glanced down at her clothes, knowing she was overdressed. "Yeah. No time to change."

"Look, we've got a ton of booze. Have a drink. Tito! Tito, she needs a drink!"

Amelia accepted the drink with a nod of the head. The booze was strong. It had a sour taste. With some luck, it had been fabricated in Pili's dirty bathtub. If not, it was liable to have come from somewhere much worse. But it wouldn't be hazardous. Pili didn't allow additives in her home.

She watched the partygoers flirting, chatting, dancing. Amelia wondered why some people found it easy to be happy, like an automatic switch had been turned on in them the moment they were born, while she watched in silence, at a distance, unmoved by the merriment. Amelia's cup was efficiently refilled through the night. Although she neither danced nor spoke much, she leaned back on a couch and listened to the beat of the music, the booze turning her limbs liquid.

A guy she knew vaguely, a rare animal trader, sat next to her for a while. He was carrying an owl in a cage. The owl was dead, and he told her he was taking it to a guy who was going to stuff it right after the party.

"Am I boring you?" the guy asked. Amelia did not even try to pretend politeness. She drank from her plastic cup and utterly ignored him, because last thing she needed was this guy trying to sell her a fucking dead owl and it was obvious where his monologue was going.

Owl Man got up. Another guy sat in the vacated space, his friend hovering next to the sofa. They complained that Soviets (fucking FUCKING REDS, were their exact words) were sending fake tequila to Hamburg. One of them had made money exporting the liquor to Germany, but that was over and the man who was standing up was now reduced to something-something. She didn't catch the details, but she knew the story. Everyone had a story like that. They'd all done better at one point. They'd run better cons, done better drugs, drunk better booze, but now they were skimming.

The guy sitting next to her was trying to elbow her out of the way so his friend could sit down. Amelia knew if she had been cooler, more interesting, more something, he wouldn't have tried that. But she was not. The appraisal of her limitations provided her with a defiant stubbornness. She planted her feet firmly on the ground, did not budge an inch, and both of the men walked away, irritated.

She dozed off, thought of Mars. Black-and-white, like in Lucía's movie. Rayguns and space pirates, the ridiculous Mars they'd dreamt in a previous century. Far off in the distance, blurry, out of focus, she saw a figure that had not been in the movie.

There are only two plots, Lucía had told her one evening. *A person goes on a journey and a stranger comes into town.* Amelia couldn't tell if this was one or the other.

What do you do in the meantime? she wondered. *What do you do while you wait for your plot to begin?*

The stranger's shadow darkened the doorway, elongated. The doorway of the bar. The space bar. It was always a bar. Western. So, then, this was *A stranger comes into town. Fate knocks on your door.*

She woke curled up on Pili's couch. Many of the partygoers were still around, passed out on the floor and chairs. Amelia took out her phone, wincing as she looked at the time. It was past noon. She had two text messages and a voicemail. The voicemail and one of the messages were from her irritated sister, who wanted to remind Amelia she was supposed to babysit that night at seven. The other text message was from Elías. *What are you up to?*

Amelia hesitated before slowly typing an answer. *Woke up with a huge hangover.*

A couple of minutes later and her phone rang. Amelia slipped out of Pili's apartment and answered the phone as she walked down the stairs.

"How huge of a hangover?" Elías asked.

"Pretty massive. Why?"

"I have a great trick for that."

"Oh?"

"If you stopped by, I'd show you. It's an effective recipe."

"I am a mess and I am on babysitting duty at seven o'clock."

"That's ages away. Should I send a car?"

Amelia emerged from the building and blinked at the sudden onslaught of daylight. She really shouldn't.

She accepted the offer.

✶

Amelia reeked of cigarette smoke and booze, but part of the pleasure was swanning into Elías's pristine apartment and tossing her stinky jacket onto his couch. She was a foreign element introduced into a laboratory. That was what his home reminded her of: the sterile inside of a lab.

She leaned on her elbows against his white table and watched him as he chopped a green pepper in the kitchen.

"Was it a good party?" he asked.

"Does it matter?" she replied with a shrug.

"Why else go to a party, then?"

She did not reply, instead observing him intently. It was funny how you thought you remembered someone. You sketched their face boldly in your mind, but when you saw them again, you realized how far you were from their true likeness. Had he always been that height, for example? Had he moved the way he did, long strides as he reached the table? Had he smiled at her like that? Maybe she'd constructed false memories of him, fake angles.

"Here."

"I'm not drinking that," Amelia said, pointing at the glass full of green goo Elías was offering her.

"It's just vegetables, an egg and hot sauce," he told her.

Amelia took a sip. It was terrible, as she'd expected, and she quickly handed Elías the glass back. He chuckled and brushed a limp strand of hair away from her face.

"Did it help at all?"

"No."

"Well, I tried."

She placed the glass on the table and walked around the living room, looking at the blank walls.

"You have no photos at all, no decorations."

She didn't mind. Her room — Could she even call it hers when she shared it with her niece? — was littered with scraps of her past. She knew it too well, every crack on the wall, every spring on the bed. It reminded her of who she was and who she'd never been. Elías' apartment was a soothing blank slate, a pale cocoon.

One might molt and transform here.

"I don't know if I'm going to stay long. Besides, I don't take photos, anymore," he said.

"Why not?"

"Grew out of it, I suppose."

But not, perhaps, out of her. Amelia allowed herself to be flattered by that thought and smiled at him.

He slid next to her, slid across that fine line she was trying to draw between affection and desire. There was that irresponsible wild feeling in her gut, all youthful need. Amelia had not felt young in ages. She was about fifty-five in her head, but he reminded her of her awkward teenage years, things she'd forgotten. It was exciting. She thought she'd lost that, that she'd outgrown it. Even if this was just horrid déjà vu, it felt like something. It was pleasant to remember she was 25, that she wasn't that old, that it wasn't all over.

Her hair smelled like tobacco and she guessed her makeup was a bit of a mess, smudged mascara and only the faintest trace of lipstick, but he wasn't complaining. She supposed it might be part of the appeal.

Slumming it, Elías style.

She truly did not know what he was getting out of this. Best not to dig too deeply. Best to just fall into bed with him.

★

His arm was over his eyes when he spoke, shielding himself from a stray, persistent ray of light peeking through the curtains.

"Do you really still think about going to Mars?" he asked.

On Mars, they would be cold. His breath would rise like a plume. They'd huddle under furs. They'd fight space pirates and save the world. Well... not on the real Mars. On the Mars of that black-and-white flick she'd watched.

"Is it that shocking?" she replied.

"No," he said. "I think you loved that planet more than you loved me."

"You can't be jealous of a hunk of rock."

"I was."

"Planets keep to their orbits," she said tersely.

He looked at her and she thought this was going to end quickly. That he wouldn't put up with recriminations, exclamations. The amusement might be over, already. She headed to the shower. But when she came out of the bathroom, he grabbed her hand.

She reached home at quarter past seven to a very furious sister, but fortunately Marta had somewhere to be and she did not have time to quiz Amelia about her whereabouts. Once the door to the apartment slammed shut, Amelia sat on the couch next to her nieces. The TV was on and an announcer was laughing.

MARS, SCENE 3

EXT. MARS BASE — NIGHT

SPACE EXPLORER, holding future goggles, spots marauders near the outpost. She hurries back to alert her father and THE HERO about this. It must be the SPACE PIRATES who have come to ransack the outpost and steal THE SCIENTIST's invention.

There is a discussion about how to hold them off. Montage of preparations, then a battle. Despite THE HERO's best efforts, the outpost is overrun and the SPACE PIRATES break through the defenses. The survivors are surrounded by bad guys, but THE HERO has managed to escape.

ENTER EVIL SPACE QUEEN. Maximum sexiness in a dress that does its utmost best to show tits. She taunts the good guys and demands THE SCIENTIST hand over the gizmo he's been working on, which will give SPACE QUEEN incredible powers, yadda-yadda. THE SCIENTIST refuses, but SPACE QUEEN thinks some time in a torture chamber will change his mind.

SPACE QUEEN decrees THE SPACE EXPLORER will be wed to her brother, who doubles as the EVIL HENCHMAN, therefore ensuring absolute control of the planet. Three exclamation points.

THE SPACE EXPLORER — the *girl*, this is nothing but a girl, diminutive and frail — faints. SPACE QUEEN's evil laughter.

"The biggest problem, of course, was that Nahum kept changing things," Lucía said. Her turban was silver that day. It looked like she had wrapped tinfoil around her head. And yet, Lucía managed to appear regal as she sat on the couch, with a few pages from her memoir on her lap.

She offered Amelia the bowl with pomegranate seeds and Amelia took a couple. "He was an insomniac, so he'd wake up in the middle of the night, find a problem with the shooting script, jot down some notes. Then he phoned the writer at around three am and the writer would promise he'd make changes. Which he did. But then, Nahum couldn't sleep again, and so on and so forth.

"He was on drugs. I was so young I couldn't even tell if this was a normal shoot or not. Convent-educated girl. A friend of a friend of my father was the one who got me my first audition and it all happened quickly, easily. A fluke."

Lucía frowned, her eyes little, tiny polished beads staring at Amelia. She was a Coatlicue, an angry, withered, Earth

Mother goddess, her forked tongue about to fly out of her mouth and demand blood. Amelia's mother had been hard, too. She watched over Amelia like a hawk and did not watch over Marta at all because Marta was too rebellious. Malleable Amelia was subject to all the commands of their mother. As in, obtain straight As, no social life, no boyfriends until there came that rich boy her mother approved of. Then she'd gotten sick and it had gotten even worse.

Amelia swallowed the pomegranate seeds.

"And now this bitch says I can't mention any of that."

"I'm sorry?" Amelia asked.

"Nahum's daughter. Some meddlesome fool informed her I was typing out my memoir and her daddy is included in it. Would you believe she had the audacity to phone me a couple of days ago and threaten me with a lawsuit if I say her father did drugs? He ate mushrooms out of little plastic bags, for God's sake. He was lovely and he was a mess. Who cares at this point? They're all dead."

Lucía leaned back, her face growing lax. She lost the look of a stone idol and became an old lady, wrinkles and liver spots and the flab under her neck, like a monstrous turkey. The old lady squinted.

"What do you intend to do on Mars?" Lucía asked, but she glanced away from Amelia, as if she didn't want her to discern her expression.

"Grow plants," Amelia muttered.

"You can do that?"

"Hydroponics. It's the same technology you'd use for a marijuana grow-op on Earth. Everything is inside a dome. They are terraforming with microbes, but it will take a long time for anything close to farmland to exist outside a biodome."

"I suppose it's not like in my movie. You can't walk around in a dress without a helmet."

"No. But the suits are very light now, very flexible." Modern-looking suits, strips of luminescent thread running down the leg. Amelia had pictured herself in one of those suits one out of each seven days of the week.

"And you can fly there. Just like that?"

"Not quite. If you get a Class C visa, you can go as a worker, but they garnish your wages. They pay themselves back your fare. Half your pay goes to the company that got you there and they play all kinds of tricks so you owe them even more in the end. But if you get a Class B visa, it's different. You are an investor. You pay your passage and you do whatever you want."

"You never do what you want, Amelia. There are always limits. I should know. I got my Mars. It was made of cardboard and wire, and the costume designer stabbed me with pins when they were adjusting my dress and it wasn't nearly enough."

There's no comparison, Amelia wanted to say. No comparison at all between a limited, laughable attempt at an acting career that ended with a whimper, and Amelia's thoughts on crop physiology and modified plants that could survive in iron-rich soil. Amelia, staring at the vastness of the sky from her tiny outpost. Amelia on the Red Planet.

"Why Mars? You could grow crops here, couldn't you?" Lucía asked.

Amelia shrugged. It would take too long to explain. Fortunately, Lucía did not ask more about Mars and Amelia did not steer the conversation back toward Lucía's memoir.

When she got home, she lay in her bed and looked for photos of Lucía. Gorgeous in the black-and-white stills, the smile broad and wild, the hair shiny. Then she looked for Nahum, but there were few of him. It was the same couple of photos: two headshots showing a man with a cigarette in his left hand, the other with his arms crossed. His life was a short stub. Three movies. As for the scriptwriter, she found he'd used a pen name for his erotic novels and you could buy them used for less than the cost of a hamburger. But at least they'd all left a trail behind them, a clue to their existence. When Amelia died, there would be nothing.

On her napkins at the coffee shop, she now drew faces. Lucía's face in her youth, the hero's face, the Space Queen. She sketched the glass city of the movie, the space pirates and a rocket. Amelia had a talent for drawing. If she'd been born in another century, she might have been a botanical illustrator. Better yet, a rich naturalist, happily documenting the flora of the region. An Ynes Mexia, discovering a new genus.

But Amelia existed in the narrow confines of the Now, in the coffee shop, her cell phone with a tiny crack on its screen resting by her paper cup.

She was out of coffee and considering phoning Elías. It was not love sickness, like when she'd been younger, just boredom. A more dangerous state.

She bit her lip. Fortunately, Pili called right then and Amelia suddenly had something to do: Go to the police precinct. Pili had been busted for something and she needed Amelia to bribe the cops. Amelia cast a worried look at her bank account, at the pitiful savings column she had ear-marked for Mars, and got going.

The cops were fairly tractable and they did not harass her, which was the best you could say about these situations. It only took Amelia an hour until they shoved Pili outside the station and the two women began walking toward the subway. On Mina, the romería for the holidays was ready for business, with mechanical games and people dressed as the Three Kings. Santa Claus was there, too, and so were several Disney princesses. Tired-looking parents dragged their toddlers by the hand and teenagers made out on the Ferris wheel.

Pili had a busted lip, but she was smiling and she insisted they buy an esquite. Amelia agreed and Pili shoved the grains of corn into her mouth while they walked around the perimeter of the brightly lit assemblage of holiday-related inanities.

"The bastards didn't even bother giving me a sandwich," Pili said. "I was there for eight-fucking-hours."

"What did they nab you for?"

"I was selling something," Pili said. She did not specify what she'd been selling and Amelia did not ask. "Hey, the posadas start tomorrow."

"Do they?" Amelia replied. She was not keeping track, did not care for champurrado and tamales.

"Sure. We gonna go bounce around the city, or what?"

"Depends if I have any dough."

"Shit, you don't need no dough for a posada. That's the whole point. We'll crash one or two or three."

Amelia smiled, but she felt no mirth. She thought of snot-nosed children breaking piñatas while she tried to drink a beer in peace.

Before they separated, Pili promised to pay Amelia back the money. This swapping of funds was erratic and pointless, they both simply kept deferring their financial woes, but Amelia nodded and tried to put up a pleasant façade because Pili had just had a rough day.

Once Amelia was alone, all the things she hadn't wanted to think about returned to her like the tide. Thoughts of cash flow issues, the vague notion that she should visit the blood clinic, her musings on Mars.

She wanted to visit Elías without any warning, just crash on his couch.

She wanted to go to a bar and buy over-priced cocktails instead of sipping Pili's counterfeit booze.

She wanted to look for an apartment for herself and never answer her sister's voicemails.

She wanted so many things. She wanted the Mare Erythraeum laid before her feet.

Between one and the other — between Scylla and Charybdis like Sting had sung in an old, old song she'd heard at a club in Monterrey, a club she'd visited with Elías in the heady, early days when the world seemed overflowing in possibilities — between those options, she picked Elías.

She had not dialed him, but now she pressed the phone against her ear and waited.

The phone rang two times and then a female voice answered. "Hello?"

Amelia, sitting in the subway, her hand on a bit of graffiti depicting a rather anatomically incorrect penis painted on the window pane, managed a cough but no words.

"Hello?" said the woman again.

"I was looking for Elías Bertoliat," she said.

"He's in the shower. Do you want to leave a message?"

"It's about his Friendrr account," Amelia lied. "We've closed it down, as he requested."

She hung up and lifted her legs, gathering them against her chest. Across the aisle, a homeless kid, his hands blackened with soot, chewed gum. A woman selling biopets — lizards with three tails — hawked her wares in a high-pitched voice. Amelia let three stations go by before switching trains, back-tracking and getting off at the right spot.

★

Only narcissists and Heroes stood unwavering against the odds. Most rational people got a clue and found their bearings. Amelia found the blood clinic. She'd been putting it off, fabricating excuses, but truth was, she needed cash. Not the drip-drip cash of her Friendrr gigs, something more substantial.

The clinic was tucked around the corner from a subway station. The counter was a monstrous green, with a sturdy partition and posters all-round of smiling, happy people.

"Who's poking us today? It's not Armando, is it?" the man ahead of Amelia asked. He must have known all the technicians by name, who was good with a needle and who sucked.

The employee manning the reception desk asked for Amelia's ID and eyed her carefully. She was told to sit in front of a screen and answer 25 questions, part of the health profile. Next time, she could just walk in, show a card, and forget the questions.

Afterward, a technician talked to Amelia for three short minutes, then handed her a number, and directed her to sit and wait in an adjacent room.

PRIME MERIDIAN

Amelia sat down, sandwiched between a young woman playing a game on her cell phone and a man who rocked back and forth, muttering under his breath.

When they called her number, Amelia went into a room where they pricked her finger to do a few quick tests, measuring her iron levels. Then it was time to draw the blood. She lay on a recliner, staring at the ceiling. There was nothing to do, so she tried to nap, but it proved impossible. The whirring of a machine nearby wouldn't allow her to close her eyes.

Space flights were merely an escape, a fleeing away from oneself. Or so Carl Jung said. But lying on the recliner, thinking she could listen to the sloshing of her blood through her veins, Amelia could envision no escape. She could not picture Mars right that second and her eyes fixed on the ceiling.

On the way out, Amelia glanced at a young man waiting in the reception area, noticing the slight indentation on his arm, the tell-tale mark that showed he was a frequent donor. Pili had it, too. They crossed glances and pretended they had not seen each other.

Walking back to her apartment, Amelia realized the courtyard kids were in full festive mode: They had built a bonfire. They were dragging a plastic Christmas tree into the flames. Several of them had wreaths of tinsel wrapped around their necks. One had Christmas ornaments tied to his long hair. They greeted her as they always did: with hoots and jeers. This time, rather than slipping away, Amelia slipped closer to them, closer to the flames, intent on watching the conflagration. It seemed something akin to a pagan ritual, but then, the kids wouldn't have known anything about this. It was simple mayhem to them, their own version of a posada.

A young man looped an arm around Amelia's shoulders and offered a swig of his bottle. Amelia pressed the bottle against her lips and drank. It tasted of putrid oranges and alcohol. After a couple of minutes, the boy slid away from her, called away, and Amelia stood there, holding the bottle in her left hand.

She stepped back, sitting by the entrance of her building, her eyes still on the fire as she sipped the booze. Sparks were shooting in the air and the tree was melting.

She knew she shouldn't be drinking, especially whatever was in the bottle, but the night was cold.

At the clinic, they'd told her plasma was 90% water and she mumbled that number to herself. When she closed her eyes, she thought of Mars, black-and-white like in Lucía's movie, seen through a lens that had been coated in Vaseline. Bloated, disfigured, beautiful Mars.

When the phone rang, she answered it without even bothering to check who it was, eyes still closed, the cool surface of the screen against her cheek.

"Amelia, I think you called yesterday," Elías said.

"I think your girlfriend answered the phone," Amelia replied, snapping her eyes open.

"My fiancée," he said. "My father picked her for me."

"That's nice."

"Can you come over? I want to explain."

"I'm busy."

"What are you doing?"

"Something's burning," she said, staring at the bonfire. The teenagers running around it looked like devils, shadow things that bubbled up from the ground. It was the booze, or she was tired of everything, and she rubbed her eyes.

"Amelia —"

"Pay me. Send me a goddamn transfer right now and I'll go."

She thought he'd say no, but after a splintered silence, he spoke. "Ok."

"You'll have to send a car, too. I am not taking the subway."

"Ok."

She gave him the necessary info. When the driver appeared, it was ages or mere minutes later and she had forgotten about the deal. Cinderella going to the Ball, escorted into a sleek, black car instead of a pumpkin. She wondered if this was Elías' regular driver, his car, or just a hired one. When they'd dated, he'd owned a red sports car, but that was ages ago.

Amelia tossed the bottle out the window once the car got in motion.

=

There was an expiry date to being a loser. You could make "bad choices" and muck about until you were around twenty-one, but after that, God forbid you committed any mistakes, deviating from the anointed path, even though life was more like a game of Snakes and Ladders than a straight line.

Amelia realized that anyone peering in would pass easy judgment on her. Stupid woman, too old to be stumbling through life the way she did, stumbling into her ex-boyfriend's apartment again, shrugging out of her jacket and staring out the window at the sign in the distance, which advertised Mars.

She could almost hear the voice-over: *Watch Amelia act like a fool, again.*

But not everyone got to be the Hero of the flick.

"What is that?" Elías said, pointing at the bandage on her arm. She had not even realized she still had it on.

"I went to a clinic. They drew blood," Amelia replied, her fingers careless, sliding over the bandage.

"Are you sick?"

"I was selling blood. Old farts love to pump young plasma through their veins. Hey, maybe some of your dad's friends are going to get my blood. Wouldn't that be hilarious?"

"You should have told me if you needed money," he replied.

"Do you think I'm on Friendrr for fun? Of course I need money. Everyone does."

Except you, she thought. She wondered how the transaction he'd performed would show on his account. Two thousand tajaderos for the ex-girlfriend. File under Miscellaneous.

"Do you have any water? I'm supposed to stay hydrated," Amelia said.

He fetched her a glass and they sat on the couch.

"Amelia, my fiancée… it's what my father wants. I don't care about her. I don't even touch her," Elías said. He looked mournful. Sad-eyed Elías.

"It's going to be difficult for you to have children that way," Amelia replied. "Or are you thinking of renting a womb? Would you like to rent mine? It's all for sale."

"Amelia, for God's sake!" he said, scandalized.

"You are an asshole. You are a selfish, entitled prick," she told him, but she said it in a matter-of-fact tone. There was a surprisingly small amount of rancor in her voice. She sipped her water.

"Yes, all right," he agreed and she could tell he wanted to say something else. Amelia did not let him speak.

"Where did your girlfriend go? Or is she coming back? I'm not willing to hide in the closet."

"She's headed back to Monterrey. She just came to... my father wants me back there permanently. He sent her to pressure me and I spent all my time trying to avoid interacting with her. I —"

"What's your girlfriend's name?"

"Fiancée. Amelia, *you* are avoiding *me*."

"How am I avoiding you? I'm sitting here, like you wanted. You're telling me you'll get married. Congratulations."

"Listen," he told her. "Nothing has been said; nothing has been done. I'm here."

I'm here, too, she thought. *I'm stuck.* Not only in the city. Stuck with him. She considered leaning forward and slapping him, just for kicks. Mostly, because she wasn't even mad at him. She thought she should be, but instead she lounged on his couch while he was fidgeting.

"I lied to you, ok? I didn't find you on Friendrr by chance. Fernanda mentioned you were there one day; Fernanda and I, we keep in touch. I went looking for you. Every goddamned day, I looked at your profile, at your picture, telling myself I wasn't going to contact you.

"I should have gone to New Panyu with you," he concluded. "My dad wouldn't give me the money, but I should have done something."

There was that scalding feeling in her stomach. Amelia loathed it. She didn't want to be angry at him. She'd been angry and that was what had started this ridiculous train of events. If she could be indifferent, it would all collapse.

"Oh, you couldn't. I was just another girl. I'm still just another girl," she told him, unable to keep her mouth shut, although at this point, the less said, the better. She had a headache. The booze she'd imbibed was probably a toxic chemical. *Radioactive flesh*, she mused. *Radioactive everything.*

But it was Elías who looked a little sick, a little feverish, and Amelia pressed cool fingers against his cheek, her mouth curving into a not-quite-smile as she edged close to him.

"You're just another guy, you know?"

He caught her hands between his and frowned.

"I'm sorry," he said. "I don't know *how* to live with you. I never did."

"I don't want you to be sorry."

"What do you want?"

You used to mean something to me, she wanted to tell him. *You used to mean something and then you* used *it all up without even giving it three seconds of your time. And I want to walk out and leave you with nothing, just like that, in this beautiful apartment with your wonderful, expensive things.*

Amelia looked aside.

"Let's go to sleep. I'm tired," she muttered, moving from the couch to his bedroom, as though she lived there.

She *was* exhausted. This was true. But it was also true that she could have called a car and stumbled home. Sure, she assured herself it was a safety matter, that she might collapse outside her building or pass out in the car. And yet, she could have called someone, perhaps Pili, to pick her up.

She didn't want to leave. She wanted to act the part of a fool. As simple and as complicated as that.

★

He wanted to make it up to her, her said, although he did not specify exactly what he was making up for: his callous ghosting or his most recent omissions. He proposed lunch, then he'd take her shopping: He wanted to buy her a dress so they could go dancing on New Year's Eve.

Amelia looked at her text messages. There were five from her sister. She was not worried because Amelia had never come home the previous night. Instead, the messages were castigating her because Amelia needed to take the girls to school and cook lunch.

Amelia deleted the messages. She grabbed his arm and they went out.

She'd never taken advantage of Elías's social position when they were dating. A dinner here and there but no expensive presents. Of course, back then, he'd been playing at bohemian living. The nice car was his one wealth marker. He kept it tucked in a garage and they took it for a spin once in a while. Once in a while, there had also been an extravagance: the sudden trip to Monterrey where they partied for a weekend, the ability to sail into a popular nightclub while losers waited outside for the bouncer to approve of their looks, but these were random, few events. He wanted to be an artist, after all, an artist with a capital A, long-suffering, starving for his creative pursuits.

Now he had shredded those pretenses and now she did not bother telling herself things such as that money did not matter. In the high-tech dressing room with interactive mirrors, she made the outfits she wanted to try on bounce across the slick, glass surface. She could take a selfie with this mirror. She wondered if anyone ever did. She assumed some people must, people who did not look at the fabric on display and wished to wreck half a dozen dresses, leaving a man with an immense bill to cover as they slipped out the back of the store.

The so-elegant employee packed her dress in pale, pink tissue paper and handed her a bag. She was on Mr. Bertoliat's account now. And though Amelia supposed 'Mr. Bertoliat' meant well, she hated him when he smiled at her as they stood by the counter.

But by the time they sat down at the sushi restaurant, with its patio and its pond full of koi fish and its impeccable white plastic furniture made to resemble bamboo, she wanted to do anything but fight. Whether the blood siphoned from her veins had also drained another part of her, or she simply had latched on to a new type of debilitating obsession, she did not know.

"I heard, soon, there will be nothing but jellyfish in the seas," she said, looking at the pond. "All the fish will be gone."

"I find that unlikely," he said.

There was a restaurant in the city, run by a Parisian chef who charged $800 for a three-course meal cooked with 'Indigenous' ingredients, plated on large stones. He had thought to take her there, but reservations were required.

When your credit card could afford such meals, she supposed many things were 'unlikely.' She supposed, with the hefty allowance he received, he could ask that a polar bear be dragged to rest on his plate after being stuffed with a dolphin. And not a cloned bear. The real damned thing, too.

"I guess it won't matter when it happens," she told him with a shrug. "Not to you."

"Are you interested in zoology, now?" he asked. "Fisheries?"

"I'm hardly interested in anything. I spend about three hours every day drawing things that don't matter and another three fiddling with my cell phone."

"That sounds the same as me. Sometimes, I take photos. But not too often."

"You had a good eye," she admitted and he smiled at that.

Elías looked rather fine that day, very polished. She'd always loved looking at him. She knew it was bad to enjoy somebody's looks so much. After all, the flesh faded. But when she'd been 19, she had not been thinking about what 69-year-old Elías would look like and now it seemed equally preposterous to self-flagellate because he was still handsome.

If she was shallow, that seemed the least of her issues.

"I should mention this right now. I have to go to Monterrey for Christmas. I can't get out of it. I'm not going to disappear, I swear. But it's Christmas and my father wants to see me. I'm his only kid. I'll be back for New Year's.

"And I'll break it off with my fiancée while I'm there," Elías added.

"Don't start making promises," she muttered.

"I want to do it. For you."

In the pond, the koi swam and she wondered if they were authentic koi, or if they had been modified. They could be mechanical. They could even be holograms. She'd seen things like that before.

Elías held out a plastic card. "Here. This is a spare key to my apartment. You can hang out there while I'm gone. Ask the concierge to get you anything you want: food, drinks. Ok?"

She toyed with the card, thinking she could lose it in the subway, toss it into the sewer. But when he bid her goodbye and put her in a car, he leaned down for a kiss and Amelia allowed it.

✶

Amelia went up the stairs to her apartment. There, on the fourth landing, she found a glue trap with a squealing rat. She had chanced upon such sights before and they did not bother her.

She stared at the rat. Before she could figure out a proper course of action, she attempted to peel the vermin off the trap. She managed to rip the board off the rat, but the animal bit her. She pressed her hand against the wound and hurried into her apartment, looking for the rubbing alcohol and the cotton amongst the mess of expired prescriptions (these had belonged to her mother; nobody bothered tossing them out, shrines to her memory), hair clips and makeup, which were scattered upon a small shelf.

"What the hell happened to you?" Marta asked.

"Rat bit me," Amelia said.

"You better not have rabies."

Amelia opened the bottle of alcohol and soaked a cotton ball in it, then carefully cleaned the wound. Her sister was by the door, but had not offered to assist her. She merely stood there, arms crossed, staring at Amelia.

"Where were you?"

"I stayed with a friend," Amelia said.

"You fuck up my routine when you don't take the girls to school."

"I don't do this regularly."

"Sure, you don't."

"Look, you want to make sure your kids get to school on time? *You* take them," Amelia said, wondering if they had any damned Band-Aids, or if she was going to have to wrap a towel around her hand.

"I pay the bulk of the rent."

Amelia opened a cardboard box and placed two Band-Aids on her hand, forming an X.

"I pay for the bulk of the groceries," Marta added.

Amelia slid her thumb across the Band-Aids, smoothing them down. Maybe she could have the bite checked out at the sanitation clinic, although that would mean arriving early and waiting forever.

"I paid for Mother's medicines," Marta said, holding up three fingers in the air.

"And I took care of her!" Amelia yelled, turning to her sister, losing her shit, unable to keep a middling tone of voice, anymore. "I was here, every day and every night, and where were you when she was pissing herself in the middle of the night? Two years, Marta! Two years of that. I threw my whole career and every single chance I ever had out the window because you wouldn't help me take care of her!"

They had never discussed it because it would have been bad to say such things, but it had to be said. Amelia was tired of pretending that what happened to her had just been bad luck, bad karma. She might have been able to finish her degree, she might have kept the scholarship, but Marta had been way too busy playing house with her then-husband to come round the apartment complex. But when he left her and Mother died, then she came real quick to take possession of the shitty little apartment.

"What makes you think you had a chance?" Marta replied.

"I better go to the sanitation clinic. Wouldn't want to give your kids rabies," Amelia said, brushing past her sister and rushing out of the apartment.

On the stairs, she found the rat she had released from the trap. It was dead. Her efforts had been in vain.

Amelia kicked the corpse away and marched outside.

MARS, SCENE 4

INT. CELL — NIGHT

SPACE EXPLORER sits in a cell. Outside, it is night and the nights on Mars are unlike the nights on Earth: pitch-black darkness, the eerie silence of the red-hued sand plains. Despite her extraordinary location, the girl's cell is mundane. Iron bars, a rectangular window. This is all that we can spare. The budget is limited.

In the distance, there is laughter from the SPACE EXPLORER's captors, who are celebrating their triumph. Drinking, music.

The EVIL HENCHMAN stops in front of the SPACE EXPLORER's cell to taunt her. She replies that THE HERO will save her. THE EVIL HENCHMAN laughs. *Let him try!*

SPACE EXPLORER is unflappable. She believes in THE HERO.

Although, perhaps she should not. Her story has been traced with carbon paper, in broad strokes, but carbon paper rips easily. And the writer of this script remembers pulling the carbon paper through the typewriter when he was a child, the discordant notes when he banged on the keys, the holes he poked in the paper so that it looked like the night sky needled with stars.

But the stars have shifted. This makes sense in an ever-expanding universe, but it brings no comfort to the writer to feel them moving away from the palm of his hand.

9

"Why did you stop making movies?" Amelia asked.

"I got old."

"I looked up your filmography. You were still in your thirties."

"Your thirties *is* old when all you do is show your breasts to the camera," Lucía said.

Her turban was peach-colored, her dress pink. She wore a heavy seashell necklace and her nails had been freshly done, perhaps on account of the upcoming holidays. Despite her retirement from show business, she always managed to look like she was hoping someone would take her picture and ask for an autograph.

"I saw what happened to other actresses. There were certain people — Silvia Pinal, María Félix — who were able to remain somewhat relevant during the 80s. But for most of us, it was raunchy sex comedies and bit parts. Perhaps I might have been able to make it in soaps, but the television screen is so small. Televisa! After the marquees!"

Lucía lifted both of her hands, as if framing Amelia with them, as if she were holding a camera. Then she let them fall down on her lap again.

"So, I cashed in my chips and married well. I thought it was more dignified than shaking my ass in a negligee until the cellulite got the better of me and they kicked me off the set. You probably don't think that's very feminist of me."

"I don't think anything of it," Amelia said.

Lucía reached for the dish full of pomegranate seeds and offered them to Amelia. The routine of these visits was the most soothing part of Amelia's week. She had learned to appreciate Lucía's company, where before she had endured it.

"People criticized me, once. For everything. Every single choice you make is micro-analyzed when you're a woman. When you're a man, you can fuck up as many times as you want. Nobody asked Mauricio Garcés why he made shit films. But then you get old and nobody cares. Nobody knows you, anymore."

It was difficult to recognize Lucía. Age and whatever plastic surgery she had purchased had altered her face irrevocably. But the look in her eyes was the same look Amelia had seen in the posters, in the film stills, on screen in a dark and smoky cabaret where doomed lovers met.

"What was your best role?" Amelia asked.

"Nahum's movie. The one he didn't make."

"The Viking movie?"

Lucía shook her head. "The Mars movie. Before the script grew bloated and was butchered. I didn't know it then, of course. I knew little. But even if the story was laughable, he could get a good angle. There's that scene where I'm in prison. You recall it? Pure chiaroscuro. You only need to watch that moment, those five seconds. You don't need to watch the rest of the movie. In fact, it's better if you don't."

"Why not?" Amelia asked with a chuckle.

"Because then you can make it up in your mind. For example, I always pretend I get out of that prison cell on my own. I just walk out."

Lucía's eyes brightened. If someone had shot a close-up, then she might have resembled the actress who had adorned posters and lobby cards.

"You said Nahum wasn't nice."

"Who is *nice*, Amelia?" Lucía stated, as if waving away an annoying buzzard. "*Nice* is such a toothless word. Do you want to have your gravestone say, 'Here lies Amelia. She was *nice*'? Come, come."

"I suppose not."

"You suppose right. When my memoir is published, I imagine people will say I was a bitch, but they were not there, were they? They didn't have to make my choices. It's always easy to tell someone they should have picked Option B."

"So, what was Option B?"

Amelia expected the actress to launch into one of her elaborate anecdotes. Her face certainly seemed disposed toward conversation. Then it was like a curtain had been drawn and the light in Lucía's eyes dimmed a little.

"I forget," Lucía said. "It's been so long one forgets."

★

"José's working as a professional stalker," Pili said, just like that, like she had found out it would be raining tomorrow.

"You are kidding me," Amelia replied.

"No. You can hire them online. They'll stalk anyone you want."

"Is that legal?"

"Nothing worth any money is legal."

They were wedged in the back of a large restaurant, right by a noisy group of licenciados out to lunch. Pili was paying back the money she owed Amelia and taking her out to eat as a Christmas gift. For now, the Bhagavad was forgotten. They could have a regular meal, not a beggar's banquet.

"Well, it sounds awful."

"I thought I'd mention it. Just in case, you know, you're still looking for something."

"I'm fine right now. In fact, I was going to say I should pay for this," Amelia added.

"You got another client on Friendrr?"

I think I'm a professional mistress, Amelia thought. But despite Lucía's assurances that she should not worry about being perceived as 'nice,' she did not want to chance Pili's disapproval.

"Yeah."

"Fabulous. That means we can go out for New Year's, right? I have the perfect idea. It's —"

"I'm going out that night."

"Yeah, right. You're going to stay home and eat grapes."

"I'm not. Really. I have something planned."

They parted ways outside the restaurant. On the other side of the street sat half a dozen people with signs at their feet advertising their skills: carpenter, plumber. There was even one computer programmer. Amelia pretended they were invisible, ghosts of the city. It was a possibility. The whole metropolis was haunted.

And she was good at pretending.

When she texted Elías "Merry Christmas" and he did not text back, she pretended it did not bother her. The day after, she went to his apartment.

It was pristine, perfect. The lack of photos, of personality, the whiff of the showroom catalogue, enhanced the allure of the space. She could feign this belonged to her because it was not obvious it belonged to anyone.

She walked from the kitchen to the bedroom and back, finally standing before the window. The sign enticing people to fly to Mars glowed in the distance. She thought about calling Pili and drinking Elías' booze together, but that would break the illusion that this was her home. And she would have to explain why she had the key to this place.

Amelia went into the bathroom and ran a bath. On Christmas Eve, the taps at her apartment had gone dry and her sister had cursed for thirty minutes straight, asking how they were supposed to cook. Now, Amelia sank into the warm water. If she closed her eyes, she could imagine she was floating in the darkness of space.

When she stepped out, she left no trace of herself. When Elías texted her on December 29, it was to say he was on a red-eye flight and he had everything figured out for New Year's Eve. She slipped into the dress he'd bought her, did her makeup, and left her apartment with a few sparse words, which was all that was needed, since things were extra-dicey with her sister.

PRIME MERIDIAN

The teenagers in the courtyard were already drunk by the time she walked by them. Instead of beating a piñata, they were wrecking a television set. A few of them hooted at Amelia when they caught sight of her, but she quickened her pace and made it to the spot where a car awaited.

The rest of the night was what Elías had promised: good food, good drinks, dancing at a club that charged a ridiculous amount for a table. At midnight, streamers and balloons fell from the ceiling. Each New Year's Eve she spent at home, just like Pili had said, eating 12 grapes before the TV set in a mockery of festivity. Other than that, there were her sister's superstitious traditions: sweeping the floor at the stroke of midnight to empty the apartment of negative thoughts or tossing lentils outside their door. None of that now.

The clinking of glasses with real champagne, the whole thing — not just the alcohol — went to her head as she kissed Elías on the lips.

When she lay down on his bed, too tired to even bother with the zipper of her dress, she looked at the ceiling and stretched out her arm, pointing up.

"We had stars. Do you remember?" she asked him.

"What?" Elías muttered.

"In your old apartment."

She turned her head and saw recognition dawning on his face. He nodded, slipping off his jacket and lying down.

"I remember. You painted them," he said.

"It was to help hide the mold," she recalled.

"Yes. In the corner of the room. That place was too damp."

"You had leaks everywhere. We had to leave pots and pans and dishes all around."

She rubbed a foot against his thigh, absentmindedly, more present in the past than in the now. Back in the grubby apartment, the water making music as it hit the dishes. Gold and silver stars. It had been a lark, one afternoon, and Elías had humored her, even helped paint a few of the stars himself.

"You printed all those photographs. Photos with an analogue camera, like any good hipster," she said, sitting up and trying to reach the zipper of her dress. It was stuck.

"It was the feel of it, of the negatives and the dark room, that I liked," he replied, a hand on her back, undoing the zipper for her in one fluid swoop.

Amelia pulled down the dress, frowning, her hands resting on the bed.

"What did you do with my pictures? Do you still have them somewhere?" she asked.

"Yes, in Monterrey. Why?"

"I don't know. It just seems like such an intimate thing to keep. Like a piece of somebody."

"Sympathetic magic," Elías whispered, running a finger along her spine.

She thought of the tossing of the lentils, the wearing of yellow or red underwear, washing one's hands with sugar, and the myriad of remedies at the Market of Sonora. All of it was rubbish, but he... he'd had some true magic. It hovered there, under his fingertips, something that wasn't love anymore, yet persisted.

★

Aphone ringing. Amelia cracked her eyes open, trying to remember where she'd left her purse, but Elías answered.

"Hello? Oh, hey. Yeah, Happy New Year's to you, too. No, it's got no charge. No, it's…."

Elías was standing up. Elías was going out of the bedroom. Amelia shoved away the covers and sat at the foot of the bed. When he returned, he had that apologetic look on his face she knew well.

"That was my father," he said.

"I figured. Keeping his eye on you, as usual," Amelia said, finding her underwear and stockings. Her dress was crumpled in a corner and it had a stain near the waist. Spilled champagne.

When they'd dated, Elías played at independence. Half-heartedly. Dad paid all the bills, after all, but he played in good faith. He told himself they were at the brink of freedom.

Now, he played at something entirely different.

"I have an early Epiphany present for you."

As Elías spoke, he opened the door to the closet and took out a box, laying it on the bed and opening it for Amelia to inspect the contents. It was a set of clothes. Slim, black trousers, a gray blouse. She ran a hand along the fabric.

"Did you give your fiancée a present, too?" Amelia asked. "Was it also clothing, or did you pick something else?"

"You don't like the clothes?"

"That's not what I asked," she said, raising her head and staring at him.

A rueful look on his face. He did not appear older most days, but that morning, he was his full 25 years, older still, not at all the boy she'd gone out with. He'd looked very much the Hero when she'd first spotted him and now he did not seem the

Villain, but he could not save maidens from dragons or girls from space pirates.

He had settled into the man he would be. That was what she saw that morning.

Whom had she settled into? Had she?

"My father picked her present. I had no say in it," he assured her.

"I guess you don't get a say in anything."

She fastened her bra and proceeded to put on the change of clothes he'd bought for her, leisurely. She had nowhere to go and nothing to do.

"Amelia," he said sharply, "you know I care about you. My father wants me back in Monterrey, but I want nothing of him."

"Except for his cash."

"What would you have me do? I was going to break off the engagement, but he doesn't listen to me, just goes on and on, and when I brought it up —"

She stood up and touched his lips before she kissed him very lightly. "I know," she replied.

"No, you don't," he said and he held her tight. And she should, she would move away in a minute. She was tidally locked. She was but a speck orbiting him and it didn't even matter now whether she could, would, would not, should not move aside.

10

The gang had once again laid claim to the subway's entrance. Amelia ended up sharing a car with a man and a life-sized mechanical mariachi. It was just the torso, skillfully painted, but he had a hat and held a guitar in his hands. She couldn't help but ask the man about it.

"It's for bars," the man said. "It has integrated speakers and can play hundreds of songs. It's better than any flesh-and-blood musician. I also have one that looks like Pedro Infante and another like Jorge Negrete. Say, I'll give you my card."

She tried to tell him it was fine, that she wasn't looking for a singing torso, but he pressed the card against her hand. She tossed it away before she walked into Lucía's house where the holidays had made no dent. No lights nor trees, not even a poinsettia plant to mark the season. Lucía herself wore a white turban and had scattered photos on the table.

"I'm picking pictures to go with my book," Lucía declared. "I'm sure people will like that sort of thing. But they're all jumbled, and I have boxes and boxes of them. This was from 1974. It was the dress I did *not* wear to the Arieles, since I didn't bother asking for an invitation and stayed home. You know who won the Ariel that year? Katy-Fucking-Jurado. "

Amelia inspected the photo and smiled. Then she looked down at the table, grabbing a couple of other snapshots. One was a self-portrait, but the other showed young Lucía with Nahum. He was lighting her cigarette and she was smiling a perfect smile.

"Can I ask," Amelia said, "you and this guy…?"

"Fucked?" Lucía said with a chuckle. "Who didn't fuck him, darling? Who didn't fuck me, for that matter? But he was married. I spun elaborate fantasies about how he was going to leave her, but those men never dump their wives. Not for little actresses who say 'I love you' a bit too honestly, anyway."

"But you would have worked with him again, on that Viking movie."

"That was after. Ages after! It seemed like that back then. Time just slowed to a standstill. Now, time goes so fast. I can't keep track of anything, anymore. So, yes, afterward I might have worked with him. Things were different."

"I don't know if things can ever be different between some people," Amelia said.

Lucía laughed her full laughter. She was old, and she was strong and steady. Amelia wished she could be that steady. She wished she didn't jitter and jump, unable to sit still for five minutes, her foot nervously thumping against the floor.

"You have troubles with someone?" Lucía asked.

"It's nothing. Probably the least of my worries."

"What's the biggest worry? Mars, my dear?"

"Mars, yes," Amelia said, blushing. She hated thinking that she was so easy to read, that Lucía knew her so well. But then, what else did she talk about? Nothing but Mars and she did not talk about Elías with anyone. Everything about the Red Planet, not a word about the man, all truths committed to her mind. If she'd kept a diary, perhaps it might have helped, but it would have been ridiculous tripe.

"Mars is fine, I suppose. We all must nurse our little madnesses. Look at me here, with all these pictures," Lucía said, pointing at the photographs. "But I was pretty, wasn't I? Look at this. Now, this was a face. Light it, frame it, let the world admire it."

So, Amelia looked. She looked at the ravaged hands touching the precious photos and she nodded.

★

She knew the lunch invitation was a trap but not exactly which kind. Fernanda did not extend lunch invitations. It was Amelia who phoned her, tiptoed around a social activity once a year, and then Fernanda agreed with a sigh. Fernanda ended up buying her a free lunch and Amelia ended up feeling like shit, and then she wondered why the fuck she bothered pretending Fernanda was still her friend, but the truth was Fernanda had also lent her money a couple of times. Amelia didn't like to think of people as walking ATMs, but that was what it had come to on more than one occasion.

Fernanda phoning Amelia was plain unnatural, but Amelia went along with it, went to the restaurant where they normally met.

Fernanda arrived before Amelia, which was another oddity. She didn't waste time pretending pleasantries. As soon as Amelia sat down, she leaned forward, with an eager look on her face.

"Amelia, are you really fucking Elías Bertoliat?"

Amelia opened the menu, sliding a finger down the many options. Fernanda took her time choosing her food and drink, after all.

"Amelia, didn't you hear me?" Fernanda asked.

"I heard you," Amelia said, trying to read the menu.

"Oh, my God, are you seriously going to sit there without answering me?" Fernanda said.

Amelia raised her eyes and stared at Fernanda. "Why are you asking me this? How do you —"

"Anastasia is super-pissed off at me! She thinks I got you two back in contact and I've done nothing of the sort! But since I secured you the invitation for that show of hers and she didn't hire you… okay, she has it in her head that you went and fucked the guy to spite her. And it's *my* fault for telling you about her art show in the first place."

"Elías is engaged to Anastasia?"

"You didn't know that?" Fernanda said.

For a moment she believed that Fernanda had set this whole thing in motion as part of a malicious plan. She had sent her to the gallery, she had mentioned that Amelia worked as a rent-a-friend to Elías. For what? For a lark? Coincidence? Did it matter? Maybe she thought it would be funny. *You can't imagine what she does now! No, really, look her up.* It had backfired.

Most likely Fernanda hadn't even thought about it, it had been a lack of care and tact.

"How did she find out?" Amelia replied.

"She paid someone to follow him."

"What, with that stalker app? That would be funny."

"What are you talking about?"

Amelia chuckled. She reached for a piece of bread piled in a basket and tore off a chunk.

"Why are you so happy? Do your realize what this means to me? Anastasia does business with my husband. If she's angry at me, *I'm* going to lose money."

Fernanda had reached across the table and slapped the butter knife Amelia had been attempting to wield. The clank of metal against the table made Amelia grimace.

"I'm not responsible for your husband's business," she said, and she hoped that he did bleed money, that if Fernanda had started this fucking storyline with her gossip and games, she paid for it.

"Well, if that's how you see it. But let me tell you something. He's going back to Monterrey this summer. His father is demanding it and Anastasia is pressing for it, too. So, whatever you've got going, it's not going to last."

"Nothing does," Amelia said. She grabbed the butter knife again and slowly, deliberately buttered her bread, much to the chagrin of the other woman. When she left the restaurant, she knew she would never be having lunch with Fernanda again.

*

She went back to the blood clinic. She was certain Elías wouldn't appreciate the fresh mark on her arm, but fuck him. She sat there and they siphoned out the blood, and she recalled how years before, he'd abandoned her, how he had not

returned her calls. So she'd gone to his apartment, trying to figure out what was wrong with him. She pictured him run over by
a car, dying of a fever. A million different, dramatic scenarios.
Instead, she walked into an empty apartment. The only traces
of him that remained were the stars on the bedroom's ceiling
and the leaks slowly dripping across the floor.

It was that emptiness that she attempted to escape as the
machinery whirred and the tourniquet tightened, the centrifuge
spinning and separating plasma and blood.

It was that helplessness which she must combat.

She could not depend on him because Elías was not
dependable. She knew that even before Fernanda had spilled
poison in her ears, even before she walked down Reforma with
her eyes downcast.

When he texted her and she showed up at his place, and
when he noticed the mark, she told him to mind his own
business, to mind Anastasia and his own fucking life because
she had hers.

How he stared at her.

"You should tell me if you need help," he said.

"And you should have told me it was her," she replied.

He ran a hand down his face. Then he had the gall to try
and reach out for her. Amelia slapped his hand away.

"What does it matter?" he asked, stubbornly trying to grab
hold of her again. "What does it matter if it's Anastasia?"

"I don't like not knowing. I wish you would fucking tell
me something."

"You don't tell me anything, either! Look at that!" he
yelled, touching her arm, the mark there, "You just go off to sell

fucking plasma, like a junkie."

"Everyone sells it, Elías! Everyone has to!"

She shoved him away and he reached out a third time to catch her.

"I'll tell you all if you want, fine, but there's not much to tell. I'm supposed to head back in the summer. And the rest... you must know it, already. I care about you and I care nothing about them," he said, brokenly.

It was not enough. It wasn't, but then, she lived on scraps and bits of nothing. She let him hold her, after all.

"Don't go to that stupid clinic, anymore," he said. "Ask for the money if you need it, all right?"

Because she was a coward, because it was always easier in the moment to lie, she nodded.

★

But she did not stop going to the blood clinic. She had amassed almost a complete new wardrobe, courtesy of Elías, which she kept at his place, but she did not ask for money. It baffled him, even irritated him. Instead, she continued to meet the occasional client on Friendrr, or helped Pili with an odd gig since Pili was a purveyor of constant and strange gigs. And the blood, there was the blood when she needed the cash.

Her life had not changed, not really. She still spent a great deal of time in coffee shops — connected to their Wi-Fi, drawing nonsense — but she also ventured to see Elías. He had many of her same habits. He did not work. He did not seem to do anything at all, although once in a while, he'd take photographs with a custom-made Polaroid camera. This wasn't but a faint echo of his previous passion and inevitably, he shrugged and tossed the camera back into a drawer.

One evening, Amelia opened the drawer and emptied it on the floor of his neat, sparse office, holding up the pictures and looking at them. He walked in, looked at her.

"I wish you would," he said. She didn't understand the last word he muttered before he sat down next to her and pulled Amelia into his arms.

There were moments like that when it was easy to forget that he wasn't hers and she wasn't his. There were moments when the phone didn't ring, and it wasn't his father or that fiancée on the line, and there were moments when she pretended this was New Panyu because she had never seen it, so it could be. It could be that the homes of the wealthy there looked like this: manicured and perfect.

Then came May and the rain was early, soaking her to the bone one afternoon, so that her clothes were a soggy mess as she hurried up the stairs of her apartment and the phone rang.

"Hello," she said. It was Miguel.

"Hey, Amelia. You don't need to go to Lucía's home today. She's passed away." As usual, he spoke in a sunny tone. So sunny that Amelia stopped and held on to the banister, pressing the phone harder against her ear and asking him to repeat what he had told her. She couldn't believe he had said what he'd said. But he repeated the same thing, adding that there was a lawyer who wanted to speak to her. The old lady had left something for her.

"'A poster,' the lawyer said," Miguel told her. "You should phone him."

✱

It was indeed a poster in a cardboard tube. Sealed with Scotch Tape. Amelia placed it on the empty chair next to her. Lucía had died in her sleep, an easy death, so she did not understand when the lawyer asked her to sit down. There was more.

"The house, her furniture, her savings, they go to her niece," the lawyer told her.

She had expected nothing else. The niece had only been mentioned in passing a couple of times, but there had been a certain importance attached to her name.

"Aside from the poster, she did leave an amount of money for you."

"What?" Amelia asked.

"She also left money for her staff. She was a generous lady. It's not much different from that, the amount. There's some paperwork that needs to be filled out."

When she arrived home, Amelia peeled open the tube and unrolled the poster on the floor. It was the Mars poster: Lucía with the cartridge belts, looking over her shoulder.

In a corner, a few shaky words had been scrawled with a black felt pen: *Do what you want, Amelia.*

Hellas, she thought. *Mars is home to a plain that covers nearly twenty-three hundred kilometers. Hellas appears featureless....*

And then Amelia could think of no more facts, no more names and numbers to go together. She wept.

★

It rained again and again. Three days of rain and on the third, she asked for a car to drive her over to New Polanco. In the derelict buildings nearby, people were collecting water in pots and cans and buckets. She watched them from the window of the car. Then the surroundings changed, Elías' tall apartment building came into focus, and it was impossible that both views could be had in the same city.

As soon as she walked into his apartment, she looked for the sign advertising Mars, but it wasn't on. The power might be down on that street. Elías' building probably had a generator.

She stood before the window, watching the rain instead.

He wasn't home. She had not bothered to text him, but she did not mind the wait. The silence. Then the door opened and he finally walked in, shaking an umbrella.

"Hey," he said, frowning. "Didn't know you'd stop by."

Amelia held up the key he'd given her and placed it on the table, carefully, like a player revealing an ace. "I came to bring it back and say goodbye. I'm headed to New Panyu."

Elías took off his jacket and tossed it on the couch, smiling, incredulous. "You don't have the money for that."

"I've got the money," she affirmed.

"How?"

"Doesn't matter how."

"You're serious. This isn't some joke."

"I wouldn't joke about it."

"Fuck me," he said sitting down on the couch, resting his elbows against his knees and shaking his head. He still seemed incredulous, but now he was also starting to look pissed off. "Just like that."

"I told you I'd go one day."

"Yeah, well, I didn't think... Shit, Amelia, Mars is a dump. It's a fucking dump. Piss recycled into drinkable water and sandstorms blotting your windows. You think you're going to be better off there? You seriously think that?"

He sounded like her sister. Marta had said the exact same thing, with more bad words and yelling, although toward the end of the conversation, she concluded it was for the best and she might be able to rent the room where Amelia now slept. Pili had joked about Martians dancing the cha-cha-cha and bought Amelia a beer. Her eyes held not even the slightest trace of tears, but Amelia could tell she was sad.

"You're going to be back in less than six months," he warned her. "You're just going to burn through your money."

"I didn't ask for your opinion."

"You're selfish. You're just damned selfish. And you… you'll miss Earth, the comfort of having an atmosphere."

Perhaps he was right that she would miss it all, later. The city, her apartment, her sister, Pili, the café where she spent most of her waking hours, and him, too. Twenty seconds after boarding the shuttle to Mars, she might indeed miss it, but she was not going to stay around because maybe she might get homesick.

"It doesn't matter to you?" he asked. "That you are going to eat bars made of algae seven days a week? That… that I won't be around?"

She laughed brokenly and he stood up, stood in front of her, all fervent eyes. She liked it when he looked at her like that, covetous, like he wanted her all, like he might devour her whole and she'd cease to exist, be edited out of existence like they edited scenes in the movies.

"Cut the shit. Come with me to Monterrey. I'll rent a place for you there. I'll pay your expenses," he said.

"No," she said.

"Mars or bust, then."

"Yes."

She scratched her arm, scratched the spot where they drew blood and an indentation was starting to form, and looked at that spot instead of him. She couldn't see it with her jacket on, but she could feel the scar tissue there, beneath her fingertips.

"I told you. I always told you. New Panyu —"

"Years ago," he said. "When we were 19. Fuck, you don't keep the promises you make when you're a kid."

"No, *you* don't."

Her throat, she felt it clogged with bitterness. The words were hoarse and she put both her hands down at her sides, giving him a furious glance.

"Fine, fine, fine," he said, his hand slamming against the living room table, equally furious. "Fine! Leave me!"

Amelia crossed her arms and began walking to the door, but he moved to her side, reached for her, a hand brushing her hair.

"No, it's not fine, Amelia," he whispered.

She opened her mouth, ready to halt him before he committed himself to something, but he spoke too fast.

"I did... I do love you." Gentle words. Sincere. All the worse for that.

The hand was still in her hair and she was looking down at her shoes, frowning, arms tight against her chest. She had not come to converse or negotiate. She had come to say goodbye, even if he had not given her that courtesy once upon a time.

Now, for the first time, she understood why he had taken off so suddenly, wordless. She knew why he'd made their first film a silent movie, a goodbye with no dialogue. It was a wretched mess to part from each other. He had cannily figured that out. He had probably imagined the tears of a girl, the pleas, and cut it all off brutally to do himself, and her, a favor.

Or he did not figure out anything. He merely fled and she was giving too much thought to his actions.

A mess, a mess. She could not even remember the names of Mars' moons as she stood with her arms crossed, her breath hot in her mouth.

"You could buy a ticket, too," she suggested, even though she knew he never, ever would. If he'd wanted it, it would have already happened, years before. But he had not.

Elías sighed. "It will be the same there. Nothing will change. I know you hope it will, but Mars won't fix anything," he told her.

"Maybe not. But I have to go," she said. "I just have to."

He didn't understand. He looked at her, still disbelieving, still startled, still thinking she somehow didn't mean it. He still tried to kiss her, mouth straining against hers, and she squeezed his hand for a second before heading out without another word.

MARS, FINAL SCENE, ALTERNATE

INT. CELL — NIGHT

SPACE EXPLORER awaits THE HERO in her cell. The stars have gone dim. The building where she is held is quiet, all the guards asleep, and she waits. She waits, but nobody comes. From her cell, she sees a rectangle of sky, tinted vermilion, and faded paper-cut moons, which dangle from bits of string (there is no budget to this production, none at all).

THE HERO is coming, he is nearing, sure footsteps and the swell of music. But the swell of music hasn't begun yet and the foley artist is on a break, so there's no crescendo, no strings or drums or piano, or whatever should punctuate this moment.

There is the cell and there is the vermilion sky, but the script says she is to wait. The SPACE EXPLORER waits.

PRIME MERIDIAN

But she presses her hands against the walls, which are not plaster. They are cardboard like the moons. They are not even cardboard, but paper. And the paper parts and rips so that the rectangle of vermilion becomes a vermilion expanse, and she is standing there in front of the ever-shifting sands of Mars.

She holds her breath, wary, thinking she's mucked it up. She turns to look at the other walls around her, the door to her jail cell, the hallway beyond the door. Then she turns her head again and there are the moons, the sands, the sky, the winds of Mars.

She wears no spacesuit, which means that it is impossible to make it out of the cell. But we are not on Mars. We are on *Mars*. The moons are paper and the stars are tinfoil. So, it is possible to step forward, which is what she does, tentative.

One foot in front of another, the white dress they've outfitted her in clinging to her legs and her hair askew as the wind blows. A storm rises somewhere in the distance.

She sees the storm, at the edge of the horizon, dust devils tracing serpentine paths, and she walks there.

She does not look back.

There are only two plots. You know them well: A person goes on a journey and a stranger comes into town.

FADE TO BLACK

ACKNOWLEDGMENTS

My heartfelt thanks to Lavie Tidhar, who wrote the introduction to this novella. Thank you to Paula R. Stiles for her copy-editing and proofreading. I am grateful for all the people who backed my campaign to fund *Prime Meridian*. Most of all, thank you for reading.

Silvia Moreno-Garcia, 2017

CPSIA information can be obtained
at www.ICGtesting.com
Printed in the USA
BVHW07s0949210718
522059BV00002B/101/P

9 781927 990216